After being rescued from witches by demons, Aaron finds himself left with a group of biker shifters to be rehabilitated until he regains his ability to shift. Once he does, due to being alone for a long time and being at loose ends, he sticks with the guys until he can figure out his next move. When the bikers take him into the territory of a wolf shifter pack, he's surprised to discover them welcoming and friendly. Deciding to take them up on their offer to stick around and build a life, Aaron accepts a part-time volunteer position at Stone Ridge's firehouse. While there to meet the fire chief, he's shocked to meet his mate—a human named Thoron Ballaro. Even better, Thoron knows about shifters . . . sort of. When he and Aaron begin navigating a life together, he learns that Thoron has a six-year-old son . . . and that Thoron's ex-wife is an opinionated bigot. Can they figure out a way to keep Thoron's ex from causing trouble while cementing their life together?

This book is a work of fiction. Names, characters, places, and incidents either are products of the author's imagination or are used fictitiously. Any resemblance to actual events or locales or persons, living or dead, is entirely coincidental.

Big Game's Flame
Copyright © 2023 Charlie Richards
ISBN: 978-1-4874-4122-7
Cover art by Angela Waters

Published by eXtasy Books Inc

Look for us online at:
www.eXtasybooks.com

BIG GAME'S FLAME
KONTRA'S MENAGERIE 37

BY

CHARLIE RICHARDS

DEDICATION

You can't finish if you don't begin.

CHAPTER ONE

"The option is open to ye all."

Aaron listened to the alpha wolf of the shifter pack—Declan McIntire—make the offer to all the rescued shifters. They'd traveled to Stone Ridge, Colorado with Alpha Kontra Belikov. Kontra was a grizzly shifter who led a semi-nomadic biker gang.

While Aaron didn't know the whole story, the pair had met over a decade before and, after a few bumps, had ended up friends.

"If ye decide ye wish to stay in me territory, we'll help ye build a life," Declan continued. After casting a smirk Kontra's way, Declan glanced around at the over half a dozen shifters sitting around the alpha wolf's lounge. "After all, not everyone wants to spend half their time on the back of a motorcycle."

Kontra chuckled, the sound deep and low, proving that he wasn't offended by Declan's teasing. "Which is one of the reasons we came this way." The large male squeezed the opposite shoulder of his mate, Tim. "One of several."

While Aaron had never seen Tim in action, he knew that the man was a warlock. He occasionally had visions. Aaron wondered if he'd seen something that ended up being one of those reasons to travel to the wolf's pack. After all, Aaron was already aware of two reasons.

First, while clearing out a facility where scientists experimented on shifters, the gang had found the brother of one of the wolves in the area—Ishmael. They'd brought him to be reunited with his brother, Boaz. Aaron had heard their meeting had gone well, and Ishmael and his bear shifter mate, Madagascar, intended to stay, at least for a while.

The second reason had to do with the fact that some of the other shifters from Aaron's group who'd been rescued by demons and the Four Horsemen of the Apocalypse from witches still hadn't shifted yet. Alpha Declan's people had dealt with that problem before. The alpha wolf's mate, Lark, was a doctor. The pack also had a couple of their own scientists, as well as a psychiatrist who they worked with to help with rehabilitating traumatized shifters.

Unable to keep his mouth shut, Aaron piped up, "I'd like to take you up on that offer, Alpha Declan." He even raised his hand, then lowered it quickly, feeling a little silly. Meeting Kontra's dark-eyed gaze, Aaron hurried to add, "As much as I appreciate everything you've done for me, I'm not a motorcycle enthusiast."

A couple of the guys in Kontra's pack had offered to teach him to ride, but Aaron had declined. Instead, he'd utilized a sidecar while Mutegi drove.

Kontra smiled, his gaze holding a wealth of understanding. "We knew you'd choose here." He exchanged a look with Tim. "This is where you belong."

Aaron nodded, wondering at that look. "Uh, thanks."

"I'll talk to Leopold about starting ye with a new identity," Declan stated with a smile. "He's our pack's expert in that area." Cocking his head in a very canine way, the alpha asked, "Any idea what sort of position ye'd be interested in pursuing?"

"No pressure to decide right away, Aaron," Beta Dixon added. The pale blond wolf grinned around the toothpick in his mouth. "We just need to give Leo a place to start."

"Uhhh . . ." Aaron thought about things he'd done in the past. At nearly two centuries old, he'd done his fair share of jobs. Rubbing the back of his neck, Aaron admitted, "I don't think I'm in the right headspace to learn something new. Can I give you a list of things I've done in the past?"

"Sure, man," Dixon responded.

"Didn't you mention firefighting in the past?" Tim arched a brow questioningly. After Aaron nodded, he turned to Declan and asked, "Any chance there's a local position available?"

"Me wolf Brahms Glowder is the fire chief," Declan told everyone. "He's usually lookin' for part-time volunteers at the very least."

"I'll give him a call and ask," Dixon offered. Then he chuckled. "That is, if that's something you're interested in?"

Aaron hadn't been a firefighter in nearly three decades, but he recalled the rush of adrenaline it always brought him. "Yeah." He returned Dixon's smile. With a scoff, he added, "I figure a lot's changed since I've done it, but that would definitely be . . . fun."

"Fun, he says." Declan's deep gray eyes twinkled as he exchanged a look with Dixon. "Not sure he'll feel that way after Paolo puts him through his paces."

"Paolo?" Aaron glanced between the grinning men. "Who's that?"

As Dixon chuckled softly, Declan smirked at him. "Paolo is a rat shifter and a full-time firefighter," the alpha told him. "He's a tough, dominant shifter and will make certain ye're ready to actually join our firefighting force."

"A rat shifter?" Aaron couldn't help the surprise that filled his tone. "Didn't realize they existed."

Declan scoffed. "Ye'd be surprised what's out there," he told him. "Got some exotics in our pack." Aaron's questioning scent must have registered to the alpha, for Declan continued, "Me own daughter is a gazelle shifter."

"Adopted," Dixon revealed.

"After I realized her father was abusing her." Declan sighed deeply, shaking his head. "Mother wasn't in the picture. Died when Sara was a wee one, from what she's said." With a grimace, Declan admitted, "She was three, so who knows if that was true. I never got the chance to question her father before his actions forced me to put him down."

Aaron nodded slowly, wondering what the father's actions had been, but he knew he would never ask. It wasn't his business. The fact that the alpha himself had adopted the girl said a lot about him, though.

This is a man I can follow, even if he is a wolf and not a rhino.

"So, what kind of rhino are you, Aaron?" Dixon asked, relaxing in his seat. He removed the toothpick when he spotted a huge strawberry-blond male lumber into the room. "Hey, babe." Dixon grinned broadly as he lifted his arm. "Come'ere, handsome."

The guy's hazel eyes lit up, and he hurried over to Dixon. After plopping onto the love seat next to the beta, he dipped his head and planted a short, firm kiss on Dixon's lips. Then the large, slightly heavy male managed to snuggle into the beta wolf's side, all the while looking happy as a clam.

Dixon slipped the toothpick into his flannel shirt's front pocket before bussing his lips over the guy's temple. "Guys, this is Helsinki, a polar bear shifter. My mate." The guy actually lifted a hand and waved, although he didn't move from Dixon's hold. "Did you have fun at the stable?"

Aaron watched as Helsinki managed to light up even more.

"Oh, yeah," Helsinki replied with a wide smile. "Jerry watched as I started playing with their new filly, Starlight. They call her Star. She's super cute."

"I can't wait to hear all about it," Dixon told his mate. His blue eyes, which Aaron had thought a little cold, lit up with warmth as he eyed his larger mate. Then Dixon used a hand to indicate the room, Aaron in particular. "This is Aaron. He's a rhino shifter and will be joining us, probably as a fire-fighter."

Helsinki's expression somehow managed to brighten. "Hi, Aaron. I've never seen a rhino in real life. Does your animal like to play?" Before Aaron could hope to answer the clearly happy shifter, Helsinki waved at Kontra. "Hi, Kontra. Good to see you again. Will you come romping with us? Dixon introduced me to Brad after I moved here, and I know he'd love to do that with you, too." Then Helsinki swept his gaze over the assembled shifters in the room, and his hazel eyes widened almost comically. "Oh, these are the guys that were rescued." His brows furrowed just as fast. "Some of you are in animal form. Does that mean you can't shift, yet?" His gaze roved over the half dozen guys who were also bear shifters. "Do your bears like to play, too? These woods are so much fun and totally safe." Turning his adoring gaze on Dixon, Helsinki added, "My mate always makes sure of that."

Aaron's brain whirled with how swiftly Helsinki fired off his comments. His attention fell on Dixon, who stared at his mate while sporting an indulgent expression. Even the alpha smiled, not at all upset that their meeting seemed to have been hijacked by the big friendly bear.

"It's very good to see you again, Helsinki," Kontra greeted with a grin. "And I look forward to joining you and Brad on an amble through the woods." Grinning at the other bears in human form—Madagascar's older brother, cousin, and rest of his shifter sleuth who'd been rescued by The Horsemen—Kontra told them, "Brad is a polar bear shifter, too. He mated with a human who lives here under Declan's protection." While rubbing his hand over Tim's shoulder, Kontra added, "If your bears feel comfortable with playing with others, these guys would be a good pair to do it with."

The half dozen bears exchanged looks before their alpha—Madagascar's eldest brother, Congo—answered for all of them. "Thank you for the offer, Kontra." His arm tightened around his own mate, a panda shifter named Zhaul. "And your wording." Congo turned his attention to Declan. "If we were to stay, we'd need to talk to you about the spells we're still under."

Alpha Declan frowned, but the look was one of concern. "Ye're still under spells?" When the brown bears nodded, the alpha grimaced. "Damn. I'm sorry to hear that." When the bears glanced at each other with concern in their expressions, Declan lifted a hand, palm out in placation. "Not because I think any of ye would try to harm us. I'm just sorry ye had to go through that and that ye're still goin' through it."

Congo nodded once. "Thank you, Alpha."

Aaron zoned out a little, after that. The others were still on the fence about staying, but he knew this would be a good place to rebuild his life for at least a few years. His black rhino grunted softly in his mind, on the same page.

Soon, we'll have a home again and a herd . . . um, pack.

Aaron couldn't wait. That was something he hadn't had in over fifty years.

Doing his best to hide just how sore his muscles actually were, Aaron followed Paolo into the firehouse. When Declan had told him that the rat shifter would whip him into shape, the alpha hadn't been kidding. The rat shifter was surprisingly dominant, and he hadn't had any trouble ordering Aaron's rhino around. Paolo had even brought in the help of another local firefighter, Dolan, who was a human mated with one of the pack's wolves.

The pair had spent days working with Aaron to get him ready to be part of their team.

After a brief tour of the firehouse, Paolo ended it at the place's small gym. "We do work out in here," the guy told him. "But it's more for appearance." Resting his hands on his hips, Paolo claimed, "Gotta keep up appearances for the few humans still in our ranks."

Aaron nodded, understanding. "Okay."

Paolo patted him on the upper arm. Then the much shorter man told him, "I'm going to go see if Brahms is available to see you." Starting toward the door, Paolo urged, "Just relax here and play with the equipment. Get comfortable with it."

Nodding again, Aaron turned to look at the gym equipment. He'd never worked out with anything a day in his life. Still, Aaron understood the need to fool the humans.

Blowing out a breath, Aaron crossed to a machine he'd seen humans use to bench press weights. He looked it over, then added weights to the bar. After lying down, Aaron easily lifted the heavy weights several times.

As Aaron settled the bar back into the cradle, a pleasant aroma tickled his senses. The masculine scent caused heat to stir in his loins, and his prick twitched behind the fly of his jeans. His mouth watered, and he heard his rhino rumble questioningly in his mind.

What has my animal so curious?

Wondering what caused his reaction, Aaron snapped his attention to the doorway. He watched as a bald, mocha-skinned human walked into the room. The muscular male appeared surprised to see him, and his black brows shot up.

"Hey, man," the guy offered in greeting. "You the new volunteer I heard about?"

As the guy drew closer, the man's scent intensified, causing a riot of desire to heat Aaron's veins. He couldn't help the way his nostrils flared. Licking his lips, he stared in shock as the reality hit him.

"You're my mate," Aaron blurted. Seeing the man's eyes narrow, along with how he cocked his head, caused embarrassment to surge through Aaron. "Shit. Gotta go."

Unable to help himself, Aaron pushed away from the weight bench and rushed from the room.

Shit. My mate is human. How am I gonna explain paranormals to him?

 I need help . . . but who?

 Aaron rushed through the firehouse as confusion made his head spin.

CHAPTER TWO

H*mmm . . . I'm gonna need some help.*
Thoron Ballaro watched the huge, black-haired man hurry out of the room. Unable to help himself, he allowed his attention to fall to the man's ass. The round globes were firm, flexing enticingly, and he would bet he could bounce a quarter off of them. Then the stranger was gone, and Thoron let out a deep sigh.

Mate.

"He called me his mate," Thoron muttered. He'd heard that word bandied about around town. Normally, it was used by guys he knew weren't actually *human*, and they were referring to their partners. "Guess I need to know what that means to werewolves."

Because I'd have remembered if I ever slept with that guy.

Thoron had never denied his bisexuality. He'd never advertised it either. His ex-wife knew only because he'd been on a date with a guy at a college party when he'd met her. His date was the one in college. Thoron had already been a firefighter.

That was a long time ago.

Considering his visceral attraction to the new hottie, Thoron pushed away thoughts of his ex, Janelle. He hadn't thought of his ex-wife sexually in nearly five years, anyway.

Not since she cheated on me.

Pushing those memories away, too, Thoron crossed to the weight bench. He took in the amount of weight the stranger had been bench pressing. A quick calculation told him that each side held three hundred pounds.

Good god. Six hundred? Seriously?

Thoron rolled his eyes. He couldn't imagine how the guy thought *that* amount was conducive to fitting in. Normally, the werewolves were much more discreet than that.

While Thoron knew there had to be at least a hundred of them hiding out in the mountains around town, he was only aware of the identities of a dozen or so.

And one of them works right here.

Turning away from the bench, Thoron headed out of the weight room. He strolled through the firehouse, keeping watch for the new guy. By the time Thoron reached the chief's office, he hadn't seen him again.

Probably for the best.

Thoron knocked twice and waited. After a moment, he knocked again.

"Come in, Paolo," Brahms hollered, obviously making an assumption. Thoron didn't mind, and he began opening the door to enter. Brahms didn't stop there, saying, "I told you I'd text you after my call. Oh." The chief's dark brows shot up as he watched Thoron enter, a wry smile curving his lips. "Sorry, Thoron. Thought you were Paolo."

"No problem," Thoron replied, entering the office. "You got a minute, chief?"

Brahms nodded. "Sure, Thoron." When Thoron closed the door, the chief's eyes narrowed. "Is there a problem?" Brahms's attention flicked to the clock on the wall. "You're not on shift today. What's up?"

"I came in to work out for a bit," Thoron admitted, settling in one of the straight-backed chairs before the chief's desk. "I ran into someone who I assume is the new guy."

"Oh, yeah?" Brahms rested his elbows on his desk and steepled his fingers. "Is there a problem between you two already?"

Thoron shook his head. "Not the way you mean."

Brahms arched a brow in silent question.

Gathering his thoughts, Thoron tried to figure out the best way to have a conversation that he'd never *ever* planned to have. He didn't care that werewolves existed. They were just living their lives like humans. He'd never seen them hurt anyone, and he believed in a live-and-let-live policy. Thoron had met Brahms's wife, Sabine, and he knew they had two kids who were grown. While Brahms had made noise about retiring, he didn't appear to have aged at all over the couple of decades he'd been the chief.

Werewolves must have good genes.

"Thoron?" Brahms prompted.

Thoron refocused on Brahms and decided it would probably be best if he just blurted it out. "Look, I know werewolves exist," he stated, rubbing his palms over his workout shorts. The way Brahms's brows shot up and his lips parted a bit was expected. Thoron quickly continued, "I know you're one." Lifting a hand, his palm out, he added, "I don't care that you're a werewolf, but I do need a bit of information. What does it mean when one of your kind calls someone his mate?"

Brahms's dark eyes opened almost comically, and his jaw sagged open further. A second later, he snapped his mouth closed. He swallowed hard before letting out a deep breath between pursed lips.

"Aaron called you his mate?" Brahms asked softly.

With a shrug, Thoron admitted, "I didn't catch his name." He thought back to the sexy lug who'd been stretched out on the weight bench. "Six-foot-five, jet-black hair pulled into a ponytail, deep gray eyes that looked a little shell-shocked." As Thoron listed characteristics of the guy, a fresh surge of arousal coursed through him. He couldn't remember the last time he'd been affected so strongly by anyone, let alone someone larger than himself. "Big and broad." Thoron smirked. "Great ass."

The corners of Brahms's lips twitched even as he nodded

slowly. "Aaron Tribble, our newest volunteer."

"So, yep," Thoron confirmed. It was his turn to nod. "Aaron called me his mate. Considering he was bench pressing six hundred pounds, and I know werewolves are a lot stronger than humans, I figure that makes him one." Seeing as Brahms still hadn't answered his question and hadn't confirmed or denied anything, Thoron asked again. "What does it mean for a werewolf to call someone his mate?"

"So you believe in werewolves," Brahms murmured, his tone lowering. "Why?"

Thoron growled softly as he frowned at Brahms. "Come on, chief," he grumbled. "Please don't insult my intelligence. I've lived here all my life." When Brahms still didn't say anything, Thoron added, "I've seen wolves while out hiking, and they always take off. Plus, there are no reported wolf packs in this area."

Brahms blew out a harsh breath of his own. Instead of answering, he picked up his phone. He dialed someone and lifted it to his ear.

A second later, Brahms ordered, "Paolo, bring Aaron here now." A heartbeat later, he lowered the cell back to his desk.

"We call ourselves shifters, not werewolves," Brahms told him, placing his forearms on the desk and folding his hands. "Have you told anyone that we're here?"

"No. Never," Thoron replied, answering honestly. "I hadn't ever planned to talk about it with anyone, either." Relaxing back in his chair, he rested his left foot on his right knee. *Now we're getting somewhere.* "But I've heard a couple of people who I know are werewolves call their partners *mate*, so I know it means something to your kind." Trying the word out on his tongue, Thoron repeated, "To shifters."

"It does mean something to us. Something important," Brahms confirmed with a nod. "Shifters live a long time. Centuries, even."

"That explains why you don't look like you've aged much in the decades I've known you," Thoron cut in speculatively.

Brahms scoffed. "Yep." With narrowed eyes, he told him, "That's why Fate grants each shifter a mate." His lips curved into a knowing smirk. "A person we consider the other half of our soul. Someone we can bond with and twine our life threads with. A partner for the rest of our days."

"Ooookay." Thoron drew the word out. He damn sure hadn't been expecting any of that. "Um, and how do you guys, uh, your kind, decide on who your mate is?"

Thoron suddenly wasn't certain he wanted to know the answer to that. The hairs on the nape of his neck began standing on end. He'd always trusted his instincts, and right then, they were screaming at him that this was going to turn his life upside down.

"We don't decide," Brahms told him. "Fate gives us a heads up when we run across that person." Chuckling softly, he relaxed back in his seat and grinned at him. "It's a pretty heady experience. I outa know. Sabine is my mate. She's human." With a shrug, Brahms admitted, "I met her two hundred and thirteen years ago, and not a day goes by that I don't thank the gods that I met her. Sabine is my everything."

"Your everything?" Thoron questioned, wondering about his wording. "What's that mean?"

"A shifter's instinct is to please our mate above all others," Brahms answered. A slight smile curved his lips. "Make them happy, keep them safe and healthy." That smile turned into a shit-eating grin. "And to keep them well pleasured."

Thoron blinked as he shifted in his seat uncomfortably. "Uh, o-okay."

Never had Thoron heard his fire chief speak of anything sexual, but there was no other way to interpret his boss's suggestive innuendo.

Before Thoron could think of any way to respond, or even

come up with questions, there was a knock on the door.

"Who is it?" Brahms hollered.

"Paolo," the fellow firefighter called. "I have Aaron with me."

"Come in," the chief ordered.

The door opened, and Thoron found his gaze riveted on the huge man following Paolo—Aaron.

"Come in and shut the door, gentlemen," Brahms ordered, beckoning with his fingertips.

Paolo arched a brow as he led the way inside while glancing between them. "Chief." Then he took a step to the left while turning to look at Aaron. Paolo indicated the door.

Aaron closed the door slowly. His nostrils flared, and he glanced between everyone. His attention definitely focused mainly on Thoron, and he licked his lips.

The move drew Thoron's attention, and even with his mind whirling with the information Brahms had given him, he felt a surge of desire to taste those lips.

Damn. When was the last time I kissed a guy?

Right. Kenny. The college guy.

"Aaron, is Thoron your mate?" Brahms's blunt question caused Aaron to gasp and jerk his attention to the chief. The man arched a dark brow. "Aaron?"

After a hard swallow, Aaron murmured, "Yes." His black brows furrowed as he refocused his gray eyes—eyes so full of confusion and hope—on Thoron. "You know about shifters?"

"He's aware of our existence," Brahms answered for him. "But that's about it. He did know enough to realize that you calling him your mate was important, so I've shared some of the basics." Scoffing softly, he added, "You'll probably have to explain that you don't change into a wolf, though."

Aaron gaped even as he nodded.

Brahms's smile appeared encouraging as he held Thoron's gaze once more. "Shifters believe finding our mate is a gift," he told him. "The greatest gift we can ever receive." His brows drew together as he added, "Yes, it'll turn your life up-side down a bit, but it *will* be worth it, Thoron." Sobering, Brahms cocked his head and returned his attention to Aaron. "Hope you like kids, Aaron, because Thoron has a six-year-old. Tommy, right?" After Thoron nodded on instinct, Brahms smiled. "He's a cute kid."

"Y-You have a kid?" Aaron whispered, sounding just as shocked as he looked.

"Yeah," Thoron confirmed softly, concern filling him for a new reason. "His mom has custody."

"Thoron, take the next two days off," Brahms ordered, picking up his phone again. "You and Aaron have things to discuss."

Snapping his attention back to Brahms, Thoron shook his head. "I have child support payments to make." He felt his cheeks heat, and he hoped his light-brown skin hid his em-barrassment. Rubbing the back of his neck, Thoron admitted, "I can't afford to lose work over this."

"You won't have to worry about those payments alone ever again."

Thoron snapped his attention to Aaron. It was his turn to be shocked. "What?"

Aaron shrugged. "Never thought about kids, but you're my mate." His smile appeared a little uneasy, but he still added, "Your problems are my problems."

Damn. Did shifters really think it was that simple?

CHAPTER THREE

Holy shit. A kid. My mate has a kid?
At least he knows about shifters . . . sort of.

Aaron could scent that Thoron didn't really want to take off work. The smell of his disbelief and unease hung heavy in the air. Still, it didn't quite cover the delicious aroma of his human's arousal.

That's something I can work with.

"Will you show me your home, Thoron?" Aaron asked softly. Unable to help himself, he reached out and touched the backs of his forefingers against the smooth mocha skin of his mate's upper arm. Turning his tone coaxing, Aaron murmured, "We, uh, we really do have a lot to talk about." When Thoron licked his lips and hesitated, something else slithered through Aaron's mind. Needing to assure his mate, Aaron quickly stated, "I won't hurt you. I'd never hurt you." He rubbed the backs of his fingers up and down Thoron's arm a few times as he added, "You're my mate. My everything. I'll always keep you safe and do my best to make you happy. I promise."

Thoron lifted a hand, and Aaron snapped his mouth shut . . . and waited.

"I know you'd never hurt me." Thoron's brows furrowed as he slowly rose to his feet. The beautiful mocha-skinned man's brows furrowed as he swept his gaze up and down his body. "Um, at least, while human. Brahms said you're not a wolf, and you're a really big guy. Uh, a bear? Are you dangerous as a bear?"

Seeing the way Thoron looked at him caused the blood to heat in Aaron's veins. He relished the hungry expression he saw there, even if it was ever-so-fleeting. Then his mate's words registered.

Wait. What?

Frowning, Aaron muttered, "I'd never hurt you, even in animal form." Then he recalled Brahms's words about his mate knowing only a little about shifters. "Uh, we're totally cognizant in animal form."

"Cognizant?" Thoron cocked his head. "Uh, what?"

"It means we're totally sentient when in animal form, man. We recognize our friends and family and shit." Paolo stepped forward and patted him on the back a couple of times. "Take Aaron to your home, Thoron." The small shifter smirked at him and winked. "Trust me. This'll be a good change."

Thoron blinked a couple of times as he focused on Paolo. "Are you a shifter, too? Or are you, uh, m-mated with one?"

"Both, actually." Paolo tapped his own chest. "I'm a rat shifter." With a wide grin, he finished, "My partner Jamie is a wolf shifter."

"O-Okay."

From the sounds of Thoron's voice, Aaron would guess that he was coming to the end of what he could process for a while.

"Please take me to your home, my mate," Aaron urged. Recalling how wonderful Thoron's skin had felt, he gripped Thoron's wrist in a loose hold. "I'll explain everything." Feeling his mate's warm, muscled flesh beneath his palm sent a burst of desire surging through Aaron, and his voice came out a bit gruff as he muttered, "Answer any questions. I promise."

"And your time off is paid," Brahms added with a smile. "If not by the department, then by the pack. You have my word."

Evidently, money talked with his mate, for Thoron finally

nodded. "O-Okay." He grimaced as he glanced between eve-ryone. "I'm sorry to seem mercenary, but" — he shrugged as he spoke — "little kids take a lot of money." Thoron's next words were mumbled so quietly that if Aaron hadn't been a shifter, he wouldn't have heard them. "Or so Janelle says."

Hmmm . . . is that his ex? Is she bleeding my mate dry?

Aaron intended to find out.

Thoron blew out a breath and turned toward the door, which Paolo opened for them. When he started through it, Aaron quickly followed. Once in the hallway, Thoron must have finally noticed that Aaron hadn't released his wrist.

Pausing, Thoron stared at where Aaron held him. "Uh, I'm not gonna run." Focusing on Aaron, he stared at him with fur-rowed brows. "You can let go."

"I could," Aaron conceded. "Or." He slid his hand down and slipped his fingers between Thoron's, twining them. "I think this is better."

Rubbing the back of his neck with his free hand, Thoron glanced from their joined hands to Aaron's face. "Are, uh" — he paused and glanced around before lowering his voice — "your kind touchy-feely?"

"I'm not normally," Aaron answered honestly. "But you're my mate." With a shrug, he admitted, "I like touching you."

Thoron grunted but left it at that. Once again, he began leading the way out of the firehouse.

At least he's not trying to pull away.

Aaron took that as a win.

They exited the firehouse out a side door that opened into a small lot. Thoron led the way to an older, gray, quad-cab pick-up. He dug his keys from his pocket and pushed a but-ton, and the sound of the vehicle unlocking reached Aaron's ears.

Finally, Aaron reluctantly released his mate. He strode to the passenger side and climbed inside. A quick glance around showed a clean interior and a booster seat in the back.

A kid. Damn.

Thoron sat behind the wheel with the key in the ignition, but he didn't start it. Instead, he sat frowning out the windshield. His other hand rested on the wheel, his thumb bumping it restlessly.

After clearing his throat, Thoron glanced Aaron's way and muttered, "Seatbelt," before firing up the truck.

Obeying, Aaron strapped himself in. "Just so you know," he began softly, watching as Thoron started them on their way. "A shifter believes finding their fated mate to be the best damn thing to ever happen to them."

Thoron nodded. "Yeah. The chief mentioned that, too."

Aaron nodded, too, recalling that Brahms had indeed said that. "Right. Well." He desperately wanted to reach out to Thoron again, but seeing the tension in his forearms where he held the steering wheel, he resisted. "I believe that, too." After licking his lips, Aaron told him, "I know this is probably coming out of left field, but I'm dedicated to making a relationship with you work."

After a quick glance Aaron's way, Thoron returned his attention to the wheel. "But you don't even know me." He glanced at him again. "And I don't know you."

"That'll change," Aaron replied firmly. Cocking his head, he asked, "Is it because I'm a man? You were married, so—"

Thoron scoffed, cutting off Aaron's words. "No, I'm bi. That you're a man isn't an issue." Sweeping his gaze over Aaron, his expression turned appreciative. "And I find you attractive, although you've never been my type in the past." Thoron shrugged as he turned his truck into a driveway. Reaching up, he hit a button on the fob clipped to the sun visor, making the garage door before them open. "Finding anyone hasn't been on my radar for a long, long time."

Aaron appreciated that he wouldn't have to fight anyone for Thoron's attention, but he couldn't resist asking, "Why is that, Thoron?" After his mate shut off the truck, he followed his example and slid from the truck. "You're a good-looking man."

"Thanks." Thoron led the way out of the detached garage toward the small craftsman-style home. "Janelle cheated on me," he declared bluntly. "So finding someone I trusted wasn't worth the hassle." Jingling his keys and betraying his nerves, Thoron added, "My right hand works fine and so do one-night stands."

"I'll never cheat on you," Aaron declared.

Inserting the key into the front door lock, Thoron peered over his shoulder at Aaron. "You can't promise that." He unlocked the door and led the way inside, bitterness filling his voice. "A firefighter's hours are long, the work is dangerous, and the money ain't that great. You could get tired of dealin' with it."

"I'm guessing your ex did, huh?" Aaron guessed, following Thoron and closing the door behind him. When he saw Thoron nod, Aaron reached out and grabbed his mate's wrist, forcing him to turn. "Well, I *can* promise that because I'm a shifter." Seeing the disbelief on his human's face, Aaron told him, "A shifter bonded to his fated mate can't even get it up for anyone else." He rubbed Thoron's pulse point, trying to soothe his clearly agitated mate. "I'll never want another. Not ever. You're it for me." With a growl, Aaron couldn't help but add, "And shifters are damn possessive, so if someone else tries to touch you, I'll probably rip their arms off."

Hearing Thoron scoff softly and seeing the corners of his lips twitch, Aaron knew his mate thought he was kidding. He wasn't, but he didn't explain that. Aaron would reiterate his possessiveness another time.

Thoron's brows furrowed, and he held Aaron's gaze. "Is that true? Shifters really can't get it up for anyone but their mate?"

Aaron nodded. "Yep." Then he grinned and added, "You

can check with Brahms or Paolo if you don't believe me." He figured confirmation from his friends would help.

"Talking about sex with others ain't really my thing," Thoron admitted, even though his scent made Aaron wonder if he wasn't at least considering it. Holding his gaze, Thoron quietly asked, "I've never cheated on a partner, but what does a shifter do if their human mate does?"

Just the idea of a human mate going to someone other than their shifter for pleasure sounded damn ludicrous in Aaron's brain. Still, his mate had asked, and he'd promised to answer all his questions. Plus, the idea of Thoron possibly wanting someone else put Aaron's rhino on edge.

"That would *never* happen," Aaron stated confidently. When Thoron once again scented of disbelief, he continued, "And I'll tell you why." Taking a step to close the distance between them, Aaron rested his free hand on Thoron's hip. The warmth of Thoron's skin radiated through the thin tank top the man was wearing, causing the hairs on Aaron's arm to stand on end. Holding Thoron's gaze, arousal simmering through him, Aaron stated, "Because one of those things a shifter is dedicated to is pleasing our mate . . . in *all* ways." Aaron decided to no longer talk in hypotheticals and claimed, "The bliss I will give you, my mate, will keep you beyond satisfied."

The draw of Thoron's full dark lips was becoming too much. Aaron released his mate's wrist in favor of cupping his jaw. At the same time, he began lowering his head.

Thoron's brown eyes narrowed just a smidge, but he didn't draw away. "Sure of yourself, are you?"

Hearing the huskiness in Thoron's tone, Aaron smiled. "Oh, yes." He'd had one hell of a dry spell due to being captured by witches, and he couldn't wait to end it with this handsome human before him. *My mate.* "With our mates, experiences are heightened."

Without waiting for a response, Aaron sealed his lips over Thoron's. He relished the heady scent of his mate's arousal as he swiped his tongue along his bottom lip and reveled in his taste. When Thoron parted his lips, giving Aaron access, he dipped his tongue inside. His human's flavor burst across taste buds, yanking an appreciative groan from deep within him.

Exquisite.

Sliding the hand on Thoron's hip around his mate's waist, Aaron drew his human forward. Having his soon-to-be lover's body pressed flush to his own allowed him to feel his mate's answering erection. The pressure to his own shaft sent tingles spreading through his body, the sensation beyond belief.

Aaron's senses soared as he lost himself in the bliss of tasting and feeling his mate.

CHAPTER FOUR

Thoron figured he should put a stop to the kiss. He knew they were supposed to be talking. There was still so much he needed to know, to figure out.

Except, Aaron tasted so damn good, and his kiss felt like a whole-body experience.

With his cock throbbing in his shorts, Thoron allowed common sense to flee. He could worry about everything else later. Instead, he gave himself over to the feel of the man against him, ravishing his mouth as if he were a drowning man and Thoron was a tall glass of water.

Lifting one hand, Thoron threaded it into Aaron's hair. The move tugged the strands from the band, allowing him to grip the silky lengths and hold him in place. Thoron wrapped his other arm around Aaron's waist, mirroring the slightly larger man's hold.

Thoron did a little exploring of his own, twining his tongue with Aaron's. He fed the other man a grunt as he nipped at the larger man's lips. Giving as good as he got, Thoron mapped Aaron's mouth, learning the other man.

Bucking in Aaron's hold, Thoron searched for friction on his aching length. The thin material of his boxer briefs and shorts allowed him to feel the thick rod trapped behind Aaron's jeans. Thoron really liked the low groan Aaron fed him, so he did it again, rocking hard.

Aaron hissed and snapped his head up, breaking the kiss. His gray eyes had darkened to the color of storm clouds. His full lips were swollen from their kiss, and his cheeks and neck were flushed with obvious arousal.

The way Aaron stared down at him with a feral need caused Thoron's heart to somehow manage to speed up.

"C-Can't wait," Aaron rumbled, his eyes narrowing. "You feel too good."

Before Thoron could question what Aaron meant—his brain wasn't firing on all cylinders—Aaron's actions told him. Aaron used his hold to swing Thoron, and a second later, he felt the wall at his back. The hand around him disappeared, moving between them.

In the next instant, Aaron had shoved down Thoron's shorts and boxers, the fabric falling to the floor and his cock springing free. Aaron made quick work of his own fly, even one-handed. Seeing his new lover's swollen prick, Thoron's mouth watered for a taste.

Thoron didn't get the chance to drop to his knees.

Instead, Aaron grabbed Thoron's thigh and hiked up his leg. He started to sway, but the larger man's hold on his neck stopped him. Then Aaron positioned Thoron's leg at his waist, spreading him a bit, while pushing his groin against Thoron's.

The heat and pressure of Aaron's sensitive bits against his own yanked a groan from Thoron's throat.

"Yeah," Aaron hissed as he began rutting, sliding his prick against Thoron's. His deep voice managed to drop further, coming out rough. "Like those noises." Pressing his temple against Thoron's, Aaron continued to rut. "Wanna see you spray, baby."

Thoron dug his fingers into Aaron's upper arms and hung on for the ride. Heat flushed through his body. Tingles spread from his groin, causing the hairs on his legs to stand on end. His gut clenched, and his nipples beaded.

"Fuuuuuck," Thoron rumbled, shudders racking him. His balls began to pull tight, and his orgasm was so close he could nearly taste it. "A-Aaron."

"That's the way, baby," Aaron murmured gruffly, speeding up his ruts. "So good. Feel so good." He turned his head and whispered hotly into his ear, "Paint us, Thor. Come all over us."

Then Aaron nipped Thoron's earlobe, and that slight sting was the last push he needed. A jolt hit Thoron as his orgasm crashed through his system. His testicles drew up as his release surged, and his seed burst from him in ecstasy-inducing spurts.

Moaning Aaron's name, Thoron clung to the larger man as he flew on the wings of his release.

"Oh, yeah." Aaron rumbled the words, his voice deep and sexy. "Sssooo gorgeous." Then he let out a deep bellow as he tipped his head back. "Thor!"

A hard jerk hit the big body, pressing Thoron into the wall as Aaron found his release. The shifter's massive tool sprayed, increasing the mess between them. Stream after stream erupted from Aaron's cock, the shaft twitching against Thoron's.

Panting heavily, Thoron slowly came back to himself. He swallowed hard, trying to get moisture into his dry throat. His fingers ached where he clutched Aaron, and he eased his hold.

Thoron couldn't ever remember coming so hard from a rub-off. Hell, he couldn't remember the last time he'd come so hard, full stop. Acknowledging that, Thoron wondered just how good actual sex with Aaron would be.

That must be why the human in a fated pairing never strays.

Feeling Aaron's lips on his temple, Thoron let out a deep sigh. "Wow." He couldn't stop himself from whispering the word.

Aaron chuckled softly and bussed another kiss to Thoron's temple. "Yeah." Lifting his head a little, he met Thoron's gaze with a sated expression. "Wow." Aaron dipped his head and pecked his lips to Thoron's. "I can't wait to share everything with you, my mate."

Right. Mates.

Thoron dragged a few brain cells together and stated, "Guess we should do a little more talking now that we've taken the edge off, huh?"

Aaron stared into Thoron's eyes as if he were trying to read what was going through his mind. Except, Thoron knew that wouldn't work. Aaron had fried his brain, so there was nothing to read.

With a smirk, Aaron gently released his thigh, allowing Thoron to lower his leg. "I like that expression on your face, Thoron," Aaron told him, easing back a step. Gripping the hem of his shirt, he tugged it over his head. "I plan to put it there often."

With his attention snagging on Aaron's wide torso and ripped abdomen, Thoron found his brain stalling once more. His gaze roved over the delineated lines of Aaron's eight-pack, as well as his defined pectorals. Spotting the pebbled nubs of Aaron's nipples, Thoron licked his lips.

"Another time, baby," Aaron rumbled, teasing his fingertips along Thoron's jaw.

Thoron snapped his attention back to Aaron's face and saw the knowing gleam in his gray eyes. "Huh?" he muttered oh-so-eloquently.

Gee-zus. This guy is totally scrambling my brain.

Aaron's smile was warm with a hint of renewed desire. "I like the way you're lookin' at me, Thoron, but if I take you to bed right now, I'm gonna claim ya." His voice grew thick with arousal even as he shook his head. "And I don't think you're ready for that."

Claim?

"What's that mean?" Thoron managed to ask. At the same time, the cold dampness of his tank top registered, reminding him that they'd both sprayed all over their shirts. "What's claiming?"

As Thoron spoke, he carefully pulled the fabric away from his skin, then tugged it up and off.

Thoron used a clean spot on his shirt to give his groin and chest a cursory wipe before tossing it on the floor. Then he crouched and grabbed his shorts. As Thoron tugged them on, sans underwear, he did his best to keep from blushing.

Aaron had already seen the goods, after all.

By the time Thoron straightened and returned his attention to Aaron, the shifter had refastened his jeans and stood waiting for him, his own soiled shirt in hand.

"How about a drink, and I'll explain a few more things about shifters?" Aaron offered.

Thoron nodded. "A drink sounds about right." After grabbing his underwear and dirty shirt, he waved toward Aaron's own. "Give that here. I'll start a load of laundry."

The activity would give him a second to wrap his brain around everything that had happened in the last hour or so.

I hope.

"Okay." Aaron handed over his shirt.

Thoron waved a hand toward the kitchen. "Feel free to help yourself." Pointing to the cabinet above the stove, he added, "There's spirits in there. I'll take a whiskey on the rocks."

That cabinet was built around the range hood, so it didn't have a lot of space, but it had room for liquor, and Thoron wanted a stiff drink right about then.

After hearing Aaron confirm with another *okay*, Thoron headed down the hall to his bedroom. He went into his closet, dropped the dirty clothes into his laundry basket, and then picked up said basket. Carrying it back to the hall, Thoron set it down on the wood floor before opening the doors concealing his washer and dryer. Thoron could hear Aaron puttering around in his kitchen as he started the wash.

Thoron stared at the softly rumbling machine for several

minutes, his brain whirling.

When Thoron felt a hand on his shoulder, he startled, swinging around. He sucked in a deep breath as he watched Aaron, who had his hand lifted in placation. His new lover stared at him with a worried expression.

"I said your name," Aaron claimed. "Guess you didn't hear me." Holding out a tumbler with ice clinking in the glass of amber liquid, Aaron murmured, "Guess you're freaking out right about now."

Taking the glass, Thoron jerked his chin in a sharp nod. "Yeah," he muttered. He lifted the glass to his lips and took a deep swallow. Feeling the burn of the alcohol, Thoron waited until it settled in his gut before taking a smaller sip. Then he admitted, "Never thought something like this would happen to me. I thought werewolves" — Thoron paused and shook his head — "Uh, shifters, rather. Guess I always thought they kept to their own kind."

Aaron offered him an understanding smile. "What you're feeling is normal," he told him. Reaching out, he took Thoron's hand and began drawing him forward. "Sit with me?"

Thoron followed meekly. Hell, what else could he do? Entering his living room, Thoron spotted another tumbler situated on a coaster on the coffee table. Aaron sat before it and picked up his drink before tugging on Thoron's hand to encourage him to sit beside him.

While Thoron still didn't understand why he was allowing the hand-holding, he didn't pull away from Aaron. He settled beside the larger male before taking another sip of his drink. After resting the tumbler on the arm of the sofa, Thoron turned his attention back to Aaron.

The other male was watching him. When their gazes met, Aaron smiled. "So, a shifter claims his mate through sex. I spill in you, marking you internally. Externally, I mark you by giving you a claiming bite." He lifted his hand and touched the flesh of his neck where it met his shoulder. "Here." Aaron's focus flicked to Thoron's neck, and his expression turned hungry, as if imagining that. Then he refocused on Thoron's face. "It's extremely pleasurable." His gray eyes narrowed as his lips curved into a predatory smile. "You'll orgasm from it . . . *every* time."

For some reason, the fact that he would get bitten wasn't what concerned him. He'd sort of expected it, considering he'd always called them werewolves. Instead, his concern went in a completely different direction.

"Uh, y-you have to sp-spill in me?" Thoron's attention flicked to Aaron's fly, and he recalled the impressive package the shifter was sporting. "You, uh, expect to fuck me?"

There was no way the guy could fit. It just wasn't possible. He was huge.

"Yes, my mate," Aaron replied, sounding way too calm. His fingers traced along Thoron's jaw, drawing his attention back to his face. "Yes, I'll fuck you." Obviously reading Thoron's concern — or disbelief — Aaron assured, "You'll be ready. I promise."

"I don't think so," Thoron countered with a shake of his head. "You're way too big." When Aaron opened his mouth, probably to counter him or encourage him, Thoron added, "And I don't bottom."

While that wasn't true — he *had* bottomed and had even enjoyed it, although it had been a long damn time ago — there was just no way that Thoron could manage a cock Aaron's size.

No fucking way.

CHAPTER FIVE

Aaron scented the lie the second it rolled off of Thoron's tongue. He also smelled his mate's fear. His mate had seen what Aaron was packing and didn't trust him to make it work between them.

I'll prove him wrong . . . eventually. As long as he accepts me, there's no rush.

Bringing Thoron's hand to his lips, Aaron pressed a firm kiss to his palm. He held his mate's gaze as he lowered their twined fingers to Thoron's thigh. Then Aaron released the human.

Aaron placed his tumbler back on the coffee table. Moving his left hand to the back of the sofa, he turned to face Thoron. He could see the lines of tension tightening around the worried frown creasing his lips.

Teasing along the skin of Thoron's bald nape, Aaron rested his right hand on his mate's thigh. He squeezed lightly as he leaned toward Thoron. To Aaron's pleasure, his mate helped close the distance between them.

Capturing Thoron's lips, Aaron kept the kiss slow and gentle as he explored his mate anew. He enjoyed his human's flavor mixed with the whiskey. His mate had good taste in liquor.

Breaking the kiss, Aaron kept his face close to Thoron's. "Shifters can tell a lot of things by scent," he whispered, holding his mate's brown-eyed gaze. "Like when someone is lying to us."

Thoron's eyes widened, and he sucked in a hard, audible

gasp.

Aaron bussed a kiss to the corner of Thoron's mouth before pulling away a little again. "Like I know that you *do* bottom, but you're also afraid. That's okay." Offering his mate an encouraging smile, Aaron saw the worry tightening his mouth once more. "I know I'm extremely well-hung." With a deprecating smirk, he stated, "Hell, I share my psyche with a black rhino, so of course, I'm well-hung." Aaron shrugged. It was what it was. "But remember, *you* are my mate, and your pleasure is paramount to me. When we get to me claiming your ass, and that doesn't have to happen right away, I'll make certain you are so out of your mind with bliss that you'll easily be able to take me."

For a moment, Thoron just stared at him.

Aaron waited patiently. While his rhino huffed in his mind, wanting to get to the claiming right away, he mentally reminded his animal that their mate's needs came first. They would get to it. It just wouldn't be that day.

Finally, Thoron let out a deep breath. "You can *smell* lies?"

"We can," Aaron confirmed. That hadn't really been what he thought Thoron would focus on, but he'd promised to answer all his questions. "The scents people give off can tell us other things, too, like their emotional state. Whether they're happy, sad, scared, or upset." When Thoron continued to keep quiet, Aaron thought of a way to make it a positive. "It's a good way for me to know if you're upset about something without you having to tell me. That way, I know I need to correct something."

Thoron nodded slowly. "Okay." Then he smirked, and his brown eyes appeared to twinkle. "So, a black rhino, huh?"

Aaron nodded again, pleased his mate was starting to ask questions.

Scoffing, Thoron muttered, "That would explain the size of your pecker."

Barking a laugh, Aaron grinned at Thoron. "Paranormals, in general, are pretty well endowed." He shrugged. "Just a thing, I guess."

Thoron's brows furrowed. "Paranormals?"

Grimacing, Aaron realized he'd opened a can of worms. "Shifters aren't the only species out there besides humans." Seeing Thoron's questioning expression, Aaron asked, "Do you really want specifics on other species right now? Or should we just stick with shifters for tonight?"

With a wince, Thoron muttered, "Yeah, better just to stick with shifters."

"Once you think you're ready, we'll revisit the subject," Aaron assured, squeezing Thoron's thigh again. "So, shifter basics."

For the next while, Aaron shared a little shifter one-oh-one. He told Thoron about their heightened senses, strength, and immune system. Aaron explained pack hierarchy and the purpose of certain positions—alpha, beta, enforcers, and trackers. Aaron even shared how Leopold was the wolf pack's identity specialist and how he'd just made Aaron's new one for him.

"Why did you need a new identity?" Thoron asked before taking a sip of his whiskey.

"There was a circle of witches that was kidnapping shifters," Aaron explained, realizing he couldn't *completely* keep other paranormal species out of the conversation. When Thoron mouthed the word *witches*, Aaron smiled. "We'll get back to that. Anyway, I was one of them. They used magick to trap me in my animal form. They wanted my blood for their spells, you see."

"Damn," Thoron muttered, frowning. "That sucks."

"Eh, it could have been worse," Aaron admitted, thinking of the brown bear sleuth and how witches had carved sigils into their flesh in order to control them. "Anyway, they kept me in a curiosity show until I was rescued by—"

Pausing, Aaron hesitated, wondering if he really wanted to bring up demons and the Four Horsemen of the Apocalypse.

Maybe not yet.

Trying again, Aaron stated, "Anyway, I was rescued by a different group of paranormals." When Thoron opened his mouth, probably to ask what kind, he quickly told him, "I'll explain them later. Promise." While Thoron's eyes narrowed, he still nodded, so Aaron took that as a win. "Well, those paranormals dropped me and a number of others off with Alpha Kontra and his people for help and rehabilitation."

"Alpha Kontra?" Thoron questioned.

Aaron nodded. "You know the motorcycle group that came through town a week back?" Again, Thoron nodded, and Aaron elaborated. "Most of those guys are shifters, and Kontra is the leader. The alpha. Kontra brought us here for further help from Alpha Declan, his doctor husband, Lark, and a psychiatrist, Gordon."

"They're all shifters?" Thoron questioned. "I mean, I knew Declan and Lark were, but I didn't realize Gordon was."

Shaking his head, Aaron countered, "Declan, yes, but Lark is his human mate. And yes to Gordon, although he's not a wolf, either."

"What is he?" Thoron asked curiously.

With a shrug, Aaron admitted, "I'm not sure, actually. I haven't heard yet."

"Is it normal for non-wolves to be in a wolf shifter pack?" Thoron asked, and Aaron appreciated his curiosity. "Or are you, like, a one-off because of the whole witches thing, and Lark is a doctor?" Scoffing, he shook his head as he muttered, "God, I can't believe I just said witches with a straight face."

Aaron grinned. "You'll get used to it, my mate." Then he admitted, "It does happen from time to time that a shifter pack or pride or whatever has other types of shifters in it, but usually it happens because a shifter mates with another species of shifter."

Thoron blinked, twice, then cocked his head. "Uh, what was that?"

Realizing how convoluted his explanation was, Aaron tried to elaborate. "Uh, so, say a wolf shifter and a lion shifter realize they're fated mates." After Thoron nodded in understanding, Aaron continued, "Once they bond, they would decide whether they would live with the wolf pack or the lion pride."

"Lions," Thoron whispered.

Grinning, Aaron teased, "And tigers and bears, oh my."

Barking a laugh, Thoron rolled his eyes. "Funny."

Appreciating that he'd managed a moment of levity, lightening the mood, Aaron grinned back. He loved seeing that happy expression on his mate's face. Aaron wanted to put it there often . . . along with the sexy sated one from earlier, too.

"So, mates," Thoron murmured, sobering. "You say we're mates, so we're just supposed to magickally mesh our lives together? Get married? Live happily ever after?"

"Well, if you want to get married, we can." In truth, Aaron had never really thought about marriage. "And happily ever after would be nice, but just like any relationship, it'll take work." When Thoron's scent turned peppery with frustration, Aaron quickly told him, "Look, I know this is a lot to take in. Finding a mate doesn't mean insta-love, or that everything is insta-perfect between them. Fate just gives the shifter a heads up that the person they've met is their soul mate." Trying to make Thoron understand, Aaron scratched at the back of his neck. "We still would have been attracted. Fate just ramps that up a little . . . like an extra push to get us to overcome an obstacle that might otherwise have had us walking away from each other."

"Like me having a kid?" Thoron offered quietly. "I saw

your surprise in the office. The hint of nerves."

Offering a soft chuckle, Aaron nodded. "Yeah. Like finding out you have a six-year-old." He shrugged as he admitted, "I've always considered myself gay, so kids were never a blip on my radar. But Tommy's yours, so that means he'll be mine, too."

Thoron fell silent, and Aaron imagined he'd dumped enough on his mate for one afternoon.

"Do you wanna order a pizza, drink more whiskey, watch an action flick, and just decompress?"

Seeming to jump on that, Thoron nodded. "Yeah. Yeah, I would."

"Great." Aaron smiled as he rose from the sofa. "What kind of pizza do you like?" Then he paused and asked, "Uh, guess I should have asked. Does somewhere around here deliver? Or will we have to pick it up?"

Stone Ridge was a small town, after all.

"*Spieron's Bar and Grill* makes a badass brick oven pizza," Thoron told him. "It's just around the corner, so I can run out to get it."

"Okay." Although Aaron didn't like the idea of his mate out of his sight just yet, he knew that was unrealistic. "You okay to drive?" he asked, his gaze falling on the nearly empty whiskey glass.

Thoron followed his focus before smirking at him. "Yeah. One whiskey isn't a problem for me." Rising to his feet, he asked, "So, what do you like on your pizza?"

"Anything but tomatoes," Aaron admitted.

"Okay. I'm confused." Thoron started toward the small foyer area where he'd left his phone and keys earlier. "Why tomatoes? The pizza has tomato sauce on it." Then he paused, and his eyes widened. "Oh, are you one of those guys who only like the white sauce pizzas?"

Shaking his head, Aaron explained, "Not that kind of to-mato. I mean, on some of those vegetarian pizzas, there's big slices of tomatoes." He grimaced, shaking his head. "That's just weird."

Thoron gave him a thumbs up. "Gotcha. I'll put the order in, change, and head down there." As he picked up his phone, he asked, "Want anything else from there?"

"Hot wings?" Aaron recalled their shifter gang stopping at that restaurant on their way through town that first time. Their wings had been excellent.

"Pizza and wings." Thoron grinned. "Great movie food."

Within five minutes, Aaron stood alone in his mate's house, watching his freshly dressed human drive down the street. He'd offered to go, but Thoron had waved a hand and shook his head. Aaron guessed the man wanted a little space, and as much as it sucked, he'd vowed to give his mate time.

Aaron swept his gaze over his mate's home, feeling the need to explore. Before he could, his cell phone rang. When he pulled it from his pocket, he spotted his alpha's name.

"Hey, Alpha Declan," Aaron greeted, figuring the man had already heard.

"Hi, Aaron," Alpha Declan greeted warmly. "I hear con-gratulations are in order."

"Yes, sir." Aaron couldn't stop his grin. "Thoron." He paused, realizing he'd never gotten the man's last name. "Uh, he's a fellow firefighter."

"That's fantastic. I'm very happy for ye, Aaron," Declan told him. "Brahms called me. Said Thoron called us were-wolves and was already aware of us."

"Yes, sir," Aaron confirmed. "Although he didn't really know anything about us, he seems to be taking it in stride without too much panic."

I hope.

"Well, I called to wish ye congratulations," Declan told him. "And I also need ye to bring him to see me tomorrow. I

36

need to talk to him about how he knew about us. Okay?"

"Of course, Alpha," Aaron confirmed. "What time?"

"Oh, not too early," his alpha told him. "How about eleven?"

"That'll be fine, sir." Aaron looked forward to getting to sleep in while holding his mate.

I guess it's sort of presumptuous of me to assume I'm spending the night.

Oh well.

"See ye tomorrow." With those parting words, Declan ended the call.

"If Thoron doesn't want me to stay, I'll call one of the guys for a ride," Aaron muttered, shoving his phone back in his pocket. He knew that Enforcer Kade lived close by since his repair shop was in town.

Aaron had just picked up the tumblers of whiskey, intending to take them to the kitchen, when he heard the click of the front door lock. Grinning, he opened his mouth to comment on how quick Thoron had been, but the sound of a female voice stopped him.

"Come along, Tommy," she said. "We'll wait for Daddy inside. I'm sure he'll be along soon." Then she grumbled, "He better be. I have somewhere to be."

Standing frozen in Thoron's living room, bare-chested and barefoot, Aaron watched a slender blonde lead a young boy of clearly mixed descent into the house.

Oh, shit. This must be Janelle, the ex-wife, and the son, Tommy. What the hell do I do?

Just as those thoughts lodged in Aaron's brain, the blonde caught sight of him. Her green eyes widened. "Who the hell are you?" she snapped.

"You said a bad word, Mommy," the boy piped up.

A second later, Aaron's state of dress must have registered, for a flash of desire lit her eyes, and she offered him a warm smile. "You a friend of Thoron's? He around?"

Then the flowery notes of her arousal teased Aaron's senses, and he took a step backward as he shook his head.

Well, shit.

CHAPTER SIX

"Thanks, man."

"You're welcome, Thoron," Russell replied. As the owner of the pub, he'd been a fixture in Stone Ridge since before Thoron was born, but rumors had started that he intended to sell the place and retire. "Enjoy your food."

Thoron replaced his card in his wallet before shoving it into his pocket. "You know I will." Then he picked up the two pizza boxes with the two cartons of wings on top. "Your food is always fantastic." Pausing, Thoron pointed the finger of his free hand at Russell. "Whoever buys this place better not change the menu much."

Russell grinned. "I'll be sure to pass that on to whoever the new owner is." Then he turned his attention to another customer.

Exiting the pub, Thoron hurried to his truck. The food smelled amazing, and it was making his stomach rumble. He hadn't realized he was so hungry.

Great sex sure can work up an appetite.

While some wouldn't think that what Thoron and Aaron had done was actually sex, it was close enough. Their dicks had been out, and they'd shared an orgasm. That was sex all right.

Driving back to his place around the corner, Thoron thought about his lover.

Damn. I have a lover. And not just any lover. A shifter claiming to want to be devoted to me.

Aaron certainly pushed his buttons, that was for sure.

Turning onto his street, he realized he was looking forward to seeing Aaron again, and it'd only been ten minutes or so. Having ordered the pizza before getting dressed, coupled with it being a Tuesday night—a slow day for the pub—the food had been ready when he'd gotten there.

I have a handsome man at home who wants to bind himself to me and spend the rest of his days making me happy. Why am I fighting this? Who gives a shit if the guy says we were matched by Fate?

Thoron wanted Aaron, that was for sure. He didn't know what he thought about the fact that he would need to take the other man's cock up his ass. Thoron couldn't imagine it fitting, and the idea of trying sure made him nervous. He appreciated that Aaron had told him he would give him time.

The fact that Aaron had backed off and offered a relaxing evening free of pressure certainly helped. It would give him the chance to get to know Aaron, the man, as opposed to thinking about him as a shifter. Although, Thoron could admit, to himself anyway, of being curious about what Aaron looked like as a rhino. He'd seen them in the zoo once, but that had been when he was a kid on a school field trip.

As Thoron neared his home, he spotted a familiar sedan in the driveway, and unease slithered up his spine.

What's she doing here?

Just that fast, the answer came to Thoron. Janelle had his schedule. Sometimes, she would drop by without notice, expecting Thoron to be available to care for Tommy.

Thoron would never turn away the opportunity to spend time with his little man, but he wished his ex would give him the courtesy of a heads up. While it had only happened once, when she'd called to tell him she'd been waiting at his house for twenty minutes, he'd been at a friend's barbeque. He'd already had a few beers and hadn't felt comfortable driving. Thoron had ended up having a friend take him home. It'd been a little embarrassing, and he'd heard an earful from Janelle.

And I left Aaron in there alone.

Oh, shit.

Pulling into his garage, Thoron quickly shut off the truck. He grabbed the food and quickly exited. Picking up a jog, Thoron hurried to the door, which had been left cracked open.

"You're not a friend of Thoron's?" Janelle asked, a note of sensuality in her voice. "Or do you mean he's not here?"

"No, um. I mean, he's not here," Aaron replied quickly, sounding all kinds of uncomfortable. "He ran to get food."

Janelle hummed. "Head to your room, Tommy," she ordered. "Go play."

Thoron assumed Tommy was obeying. His son was a good kid, after all. Reaching the door, he pushed it open, preparing to call out. Instead, Thoron froze at the scene before him.

"How long do we have before he gets here, handsome?" Janelle crooned. She rested one hand on Aaron's bare chest, and with her other, she was circling his nipple with her fake nail. "A little time, I hope."

Aaron held a tumbler in each hand. His face appeared a little pale, and his eyes were wide. As Thoron watched, Aaron even backed up a step, but Janelle followed him.

A burst of unreasonable jealousy surged through Thoron, and anger curdled in his gut.

"I-I'm not sure," Aaron responded, shimmying sideways between the sofa and the coffee table in a clear attempt to get away from her questing hands. "Just gonna—"

Unable to rein in his temper, Thoron stalked into the house. "*No* was the answer to both of your questions," he declared, catching both their attentions.

Aaron looked so damn relieved, while Janelle flushed a little, perhaps in embarrassment. She couldn't hide her disappointment swiftly enough, though. Thoron had seen it flash there and gone in her green eyes.

"Hey, Thor," Janelle greeted with fake sweetness in her voice. "I was just introducing myself to your friend here."

Setting the boxes on the side table, along with his keys, wallet, and phone, Aaron continued to frown at Janelle. There had been a time when he'd fallen for that look and tone — hook, line, and sinker. But that hadn't worked in years.

"He's not my friend," Thoron declared.

While Aaron's eyes widened, Janelle furrowed her brows in obvious confusion.

"Aaron is my lover." The green-eyed, angry monster made it so easy to speak without thinking. "And he's gay, so not interested in what you were about to offer."

Aaron's wide smile caused Thoron's heart to stutter in his chest. The man looked so damn happy to be claimed. That expression caused Thoron's ire to ease, and he was able to begin breathing easier again.

Janelle's eyes narrowed. A look of disgust twisted her features as she glanced between them. "Your *lover*?" She curled her lip. "What?"

"We're divorced, Janelle," Thoron reminded her, moving toward Aaron's side. "You didn't really think I was celibate, did you?" Taking his tumbler from Aaron — he knew it was his because it still had ice in it — Thoron murmured his thanks before refocusing on Janelle. "You moved on a long time ago, Janelle. In fact, you moved on before our divorce." He usually didn't dig at her about her affair, but seeing her come onto Aaron while in Thoron's home, he just couldn't seem to help himself. "Now then, what time should I expect you to pick up Tommy tomorrow?"

Even though Janelle was rarely on time, Thoron liked to get an estimate. As he waited for her answer, he finished his whiskey.

To Thoron's surprise, Janelle snarled, "You're *not* gay, Thoron." Glaring, she rested one hand on her hip while flailing her hand back and forth, indicating them. "What is this nonsense?"

The move caused her low-cut blouse to gape, showing off the tops of her tits. She appeared to be wearing clothes either meant for a date or to go clubbing. Thoron didn't know which and didn't care.

Janelle's words, however . . . those Thoron cared about. "I'm bisexual," he reminded her. "You knew that when we started dating years ago."

"No, you were confused," Janelle insisted.

Scoffing, Thoron stared at her as disbelief filled him. "When we met, I was dating a guy." That same guy had dumped him the next day for — ironically — a different guy he'd met at that same party.

At least he dumped me and didn't cheat on me.

"That was just a little experiment," Janelle insisted, resting her second hand on her hips. "Once you met me, you realized it was a mistake and you weren't into guys." Lifting her chin in a haughty manner, Janelle asked, "So what's really going on? Are you mad because I didn't call first?"

Is she for real?

Shaking his head, Thoron heaved a sigh. "Look, I don't care what you think." He was tired of the conversation already. "Just let me know when you think you're coming tomorrow. My food is getting cold."

"No." Janelle stomped her foot like a toddler. "I demand to know what's really going on."

Thoron figured seeing was believing. Turning, he reached up and gripped Aaron's nape in his free hand. With the slightest of tugs, Thoron drew the bigger man's head down. He kept the kiss short and reasonably chaste, but he couldn't resist slipping his tongue in for a few seconds to taste his lover . . . just a little.

Aaron truly tasted too damn good, and he was impossible to resist.

Janelle's screech interrupted them.

Thoron broke the kiss just as she swung a hand to slap him,

but Aaron moved faster. While using his hold on Thoron's bicep to move him out of the way, he took a step forward and accepted the hit himself. The blow landed on Aaron's upper arm with a resounding crack.

"You bastard," Janelle screamed. "Is that why you couldn't get it up for me enough?" She swung her arm again, trying to reach Thoron. This time, she curled her hands into claws. "Why you could never satisfy me?" Aaron moved between them once more, and her blow left five bleeding rows across his chest. "No wonder I had to go looking elsewhere. My affair is your fault."

When Janelle tried a third attack, Aaron had obviously had enough. He caught her arm and spun her. With his increased strength, Aaron easily subdued her with her hands behind her back.

"Think we should call the police?" Aaron asked over his shoulder.

Thoron snapped out of his shock, having not expected her violence. "Uh, no," he murmured, shaking his head. "I just want her to leave."

"Fine," Janelle declared, a coldness filling her eyes. "Tommy, it's time to go," she hollered. Then she whispered, "You're *never* going to see him again, degenerate."

"And now I'm going to call the police," Thoron stated, quickly changing his mind at that threat. "Don't let her leave with him."

"Daddy!"

Hearing Tommy's call gave Thoron just enough warning to crouch and catch his running son. "Hey, buddy." On instinct, because he'd done it a hundred times before, Thoron picked up his son and swung him in a circle. "How ya doin', little man?"

Fortunately, Aaron moved himself and Janelle out of the way in time.

"Put Tommy down this instant," Janelle ordered as she wriggled in Aaron's grip. "He's not staying." She tried to stomp her high heel on Aaron's bare foot, but he moved too quickly. "Let go of me, faggot."

Ignoring her, Thoron put Tommy back on his feet. "Head back to your room for a few minutes, buddy." He tousled his son's black curls. "I gotta talk to Mommy. She's a little upset."

Tommy looked uncertain, glancing between them with worry in his brown eyes.

"No, Tommy," Janelle countered. "We're *leaving*."

"It's okay, Tommy." Thoron cradled the back of his son's head. "Mommy was mean to my friend, so we gotta talk a little first." He turned Tommy and gave his shoulder a squeeze. "I'll be in to get you soon."

Fortunately, Tommy took off, ignoring Janelle's screeches.

"Knock, knock, Thoron," a deep voice called from the front door. Turning, Thoron spotted Deputy Goliath Dickman standing in the still-open door. "I'm afraid I got a domestic disturbance call from your neighbor." The deputy took in the situation at a glance, and his brown eyes narrowed. "Care to explain what's going on?"

God, there's a loaded question.

CHAPTER SEVEN

"These delinquents are holding me and my son hostage," Janelle declared dramatically, a whine in her voice. "Please, help me."

Aaron didn't recognize the man in the deputy's uniform, but he knew he was pack. Everyone who worked for the sheriff's department was either a paranormal or was mated to one. Considering the scent of human and wolf, and the fact that Aaron had met Khan's mate—a wolf shifter who'd been part of Kontra's pack, too—he figured this was Goliath.

He certainly lives up to his name.

The human was, in a word, *huge*. He even topped Aaron's six-foot-five height by several inches.

Wow.

"Hi, Deputy Goliath," Thoron greeted, confirming the man's identity. "This is my ex-wife, Janelle. She came over to drop off my son, Tommy, to visit." Rubbing the back of his neck with unease, Thoron continued, "When she realized I was dating a man, she went a little, uh, crazy."

Sneering, Janelle denied it. "I did not. You're faggots, and I won't have you near my son."

Once more, Janelle tried to wrench from Aaron's grip, and seeing as the police officer was there, he let her go.

"Finally," Janelle snarled. She immediately began rushing toward the hall, calling Tommy's name. Thoron quickly slipped in front of her, blocking the hall and access to his son. "Get out of my way, abomination." Janelle started to lift her hand as if to strike him but must have thought better of it, for she lowered it just as quickly. "You can't keep me from Tommy. You don't have custody."

Goliath pointed at Aaron's chest. "She do that to you?"

Aaron peered down at the scratches on his chest. "Yeah." They'd stopped hurting, and he knew they were healing quickly. "Raked me with her nails when I wouldn't let her hit Thoron." If they hadn't been so deep, they would have been gone already.

Guess that was a good thing, after all.

"I'll take a quick picture," Goliath told him, pulling out his phone. As he snapped a couple, he asked, "You want to press charges?"

"Yeah," Aaron replied. With a glance at Thoron, he added, "I'll probably drop 'em tomorrow, but we need her out of here for the evening." Returning his attention to Goliath, he added, "Gonna ask Declan for advice 'cause she's threatening to keep Tommy from Thoron since he's my mate and all."

Goliath's dark brows twitched just a little, telling Aaron that he understood the reference. "Gotcha." After tucking his phone into his jacket, Goliath turned to Janelle while pulling out his cuffs. "Okay, ma'am. Hands behind your back, please."

"What?" Janelle screamed. "You're taking *their* side?" She began to rush toward the door, obviously thinking of fleeing.

Before Janelle reached the door, Goliath had caught and subdued her.

"You'll pay for this," Janelle threatened. "I'll have your badge, faggot-lover."

"Ma'am, I am a faggot," Goliath responded, his deep voice rumbling from his chest. "And now I'm adding resisting arrest to your crimes." He glanced over his shoulder at them and reminded, "I'll need both your statements tomorrow, guys."

"Of course, deputy," Aaron assured as Thoron nodded. He followed the pair to the door. It wasn't until he'd closed and locked it that the sound of Janelle's slurs and threats could no longer be heard. Turning, Aaron rested his back against the door and pinned a heated look on a clearly shell-shocked Thoron. "You claimed me as your lover."

Aaron's arousal surged anew at that recollection.

Thoron glanced toward the hall, then refocused on Aaron. "Yeah. Uh, she was touching you." Rubbing a hand over his bald head, he frowned as he muttered, "You clearly didn't like it, but she wasn't taking the hint, and" — Thoron paused and shrugged — "I just saw red, Aaron. I didn't like her touching you, and it pissed me off."

Pushing off the door, Aaron stalked across the room. "The shifter isn't the only possessive one in the relationship, Thoron," he rumbled, pulling Thoron into his arms.

Dipping his head, Aaron sealed his lips over Thoron's. He'd just pushed his tongue past his mate's lips when the sound of a child making *vroom, vroom* noises reached his sensitive shifter ears. As much as Aaron wanted to ravish his mate, he eased the kiss to an end.

Child in the house, after all.

"So, we have Tommy for the night," Aaron reminded, seeing Thoron's confused look. His mate's eyes widened as he glanced toward the hallway, and Aaron couldn't help but grin, liking that he'd caused Thoron to forget. "Why don't you go get him?" Aaron eased his arms from around his lover. "Think he'll be interested in pizza?"

Thoron scoffed. "Does a bear shit in the woods?"

Aaron tipped his head back and laughed.

Right. What kid doesn't like pizza?

Easing away from Aaron, Thoron glanced toward the door before asking, "How'd you get the deputy to take Janelle so fast?" With his confusion clear, he commented, "We barely had to say anything."

Smiling, Aaron explained, "Goliath is pack, so when I mentioned that you're my mate and I'll need to talk to Declan about her threats, he got it." He gripped Thoron's hand in his own and squeezed. "She'll cool her heels in jail this evening, and tomorrow, we'll go see Declan." Shaking his head, Aaron vowed, "There's no way we'll allow your bigoted ex to steal your son from you. The pack will help."

"Wow," Thoron murmured in surprise. "So the pack is like one big extended family?"

Aaron nodded. "Yup. They'll have our back through this."

"Thanks," Thoron murmured before turning away.

As Thoron headed down the hall, Aaron grabbed the pizza and wings and took them to the coffee table. He thought about heading to the dining room but figured they would eat while watching a movie. Aaron set them down, then headed to the kitchen.

When getting drinks earlier, Aaron had taken his time checking out where everything was. He easily located the paper plates and napkins and took them to the coffee table, too. Picking up the tumblers once more, Aaron returned to the kitchen and refilled both their drinks.

It occurred to Aaron that Thoron might not drink in front of his kid, but if that ended up being the case, he would down them both himself. It would take a hell of a lot more than a few fingers of whiskey to get him inebriated. Hearing a bedroom door open, Aaron turned, girding up his courage to meet his mate's son.

Thoron strode down the hall holding Tommy's hand. The youngster looked at Aaron with wide eyes, his head tipping up and up.

Hoping to make it easier on Tommy, Aaron settled on the sofa. "Hey, Tommy. Your dad's told me so much about you," he greeted with a smile and a lie. He would remedy that soon enough. "It's so nice to meet you." Resting his forearms on his thighs, Aaron waved toward the food. "I hear you like pizza. You gonna join us for guys' night?"

"Hi," Tommy murmured, sounding shy. Then he glanced toward the pizza before refocusing on Aaron, furrowing his little brows. "What's guys' night?"

Aaron grinned. "Well, that's where us guys get together to hang out, eat pizza, watch movies, and burp real loud without a girl telling us to cut it out."

"Really?" Tommy's brown eyes, so similar to his father's, got real wide. He tipped his chin up to look at Thoron. "Really?"

As Aaron had been explaining, Thoron's lips had begun to part, and he began giving off the scents of surprise and disbelief. When Tommy peered up at him, he instantly cleared the look and grinned at his son.

"Yep," Thoron agreed. Releasing Tommy's hand, he tousled his black curls and told him, "But the burping is only aloud when it's just us guys. Don't forget."

"I won't," Tommy cried excitedly. "Yay, pizza!"

Tommy rushed across the room and stood next to the coffee table, bouncing on his toes. His attention was riveted on the boxes.

Even Aaron knew what that meant. "Let's get ya set up here, buddy." He opened a box, finding the three-meat inside.

"Ewww, mushrooms." Tommy made a face.

"I'll pick 'em off for ya so you don't have to eat them," Aaron offered. "I'm weird. I like mushrooms."

Tommy looked at him like he was nuts, as only a toddler could.

With a laugh, Aaron opened the second box with a flourish. "Or, you can have a piece of this barbeque chicken pizza. No mushrooms on it."

Glancing between the two pies, Tommy looked conflicted. "Chicken on pizza?" The cute guy sounded confused as hell.

"Sorry, I didn't get a plain pepperoni, little man," Thoron called from the kitchen. "I didn't know you were comin' to guys' night."

Tommy shrugged his little shoulders. "Can I try one of each?"

"Sure can." Aaron quickly placed a piece of each onto a doubled-up paper plate. Sliding it toward Tommy, he offered, "Here ya go."

"You said you were gonna pick off the mushrooms," Tommy reminded.

"Right. Sorry."

Aaron quickly placed a piece of the three-meat on his own plate. Then he did as he'd said and used a fork to hunt down every offending mushroom on Tommy's slice. He piled them onto his own piece before passing the plate to Tommy once more.

"Here's some milk," Thoron stated, placing a blue sippy cup covered in clouds and airplanes on the coffee table. After picking up his tumbler of whiskey and taking a sip, Thoron turned his attention to the TV. "So, what should we watch?"

With Tommy there, the violent action flick was out. Instead, they settled on the first *Shrek* movie. While it was a cartoon with plenty of silliness for Tommy, there were enough hidden adult innuendos to make it enjoyable for Thoron and Aaron.

Plus, Aaron had never seen it before. It'd come out while he'd been held captive. He found himself laughing on more than one occasion.

After eating their fill of pizza, Thoron had paused the movie to refresh their drinks. They'd all ended up on the sofa. Thoron sat in the middle with Tommy leaning into his left side. Aaron sat to his mate's right, his arm over the back of the sofa, allowing him to tease his fingertips over Thoron's nape. Touching his mate felt as natural as breathing, and Aaron couldn't get enough of it.

It helped that every time Aaron traced over Thoron's skin,

his mate shot a small smile his way.

Yeah, I have it bad already.

When the credits rolled, Thoron muted the TV and murmured, "I need to get him to bed."

That was when Aaron noticed Tommy had conked out against his father. He eyed the small human and smiled. The cutie had been easy to get along with, his antics were cute, and his big smile had been infectious. Aaron could see himself caring for Tommy just as much as his father, just in a different way.

After rising, Tommy in his arms, Thoron peered down at Aaron. "You stayin'?" he whispered.

"You tell me, Thoron," Aaron answered softly. "I don't have a car, but I can get a lift if you want me to leave." When Thoron appeared indecisive, Aaron told him, "I'd much rather stay, my mate."

"Head to my bedroom," Thoron ordered. "There's a spare new toothbrush in the drawer. I'll be in shortly."

Aaron nodded as he rose. "I'll clean up out here first, then do just that," he told him as anticipation surged through him. While Aaron knew bonding wasn't on the table that evening, he would take any opportunity to spend time with his mate.

As Thoron disappeared down the hall and into Tommy's room, Aaron put the living room and kitchen to rights. The nice thing about pizza and wings was that it was easy cleanup. It only took him a couple of minutes to throw away boxes, used plates, wing-bones, and Tommy's unwanted crusts. Aaron rinsed the tumblers, silverware, and Tommy's sippy cup, leaving them in the sink.

After washing his hands, Aaron headed to Thoron's bedroom. He made quick work of cleaning up for the night. For a second, Aaron paused beside the bed, hesitating.

Then Aaron stripped his jeans and draped them over the back of a chair to re-wear the next day. In the buff, he slid between the sheets. Aaron brought the blanket up to his waist, rested one hand behind his head, and waited.

Soon enough, Thoron was joining him. His lover's eyes widened as he slid in beside him. "You're nude."

"I don't wear underwear, so yeah." Aaron glanced toward the cracked door. "Should I borrow sweats or shorts or something, uh, just in case Tommy comes in?"

Thoron winced. "As much as I like you like that, yeah. I'll get you something." He rose and headed to his dresser. After pulling out a pair of gym shorts, Thoron tossed them to him.

Aaron pulled them on and climbed back into bed. After turning out the bedside lamp, he pulled his mate into his arms. Ignoring his hard dick, Aaron pressed a kiss to Thoron's lips before whispering, "Good night, my mate."

Then Aaron curled around Thoron, spooning behind him, and held his mate as he fell asleep.

CHAPTER EIGHT

"This is where ye saw us?"

Peering at the map spread out on Alpha Declan's desk, Thoron nodded. "Yeah." He noted the alpha's surprised expression and admitted, "I like to hike off the trails to keep up my cardio. Around Laremie's Rock is pretty rugged terrain."

"Aye, that it is," Declan agreed. Smirking, he admitted, "That's why me wolves feel so comfortable frolickin' up there. It's not close to any trails." Arching one eyebrow, the dark-skinned shifter asked, "How long have ye known?"

"Uhhh." Thoron thought back to the first few times he'd spotted the wolves. "I noticed several wolves in that area around eight years ago." When Declan's brows shot up, Thoron explained, "I didn't realize they were shifters at first. I just thought there was an undocumented wolf pack in the area. I came back repeatedly over the next couple of years to watch them. I'd climb a pine, sit in its branches with binoculars, and check out the area." Rubbing the back of his neck, Thoron admitted, "It was about six years ago that I watched one change into a man." He cleared his throat. "I recognized him as Frederick Drunger, the guy who owns the tattoo shop in town. Then another wolf changed into his brother, Frankie." With a scoff, Thoron murmured, "Man, I just about fell out of the tree that day."

"And ye never said anything to anyone, and ye kept comin' back?"

Thoron nodded. "I wondered if they were an aberration or if there were more." He barked a laugh as he recalled the last occasion he'd purposefully looked for them. "I used to watch for you on full moons because, you know, werewolves." Spotting Declan's smirk, Thoron shrugged. "Assumptions, I know. Anyway, when I saw a big group of about sixty-plus wolves running on a full moon, I knew the Drunger brothers weren't an aberration, and you guys had a huge pack. As I watched, a little cub fell and seemed to hurt herself. She shifted back to human form and cried, cradling her arm." Meeting Declan's gray eyes, Thoron stated, "I saw you. You changed from wolf to man in the blink of an eye. You held her, soothed her, then encouraged her to turn back into her wolf. You handed her off to a pale blond wolf, who gripped her pup form's scruff and carried her away." Thoron touched the back of his neck, indicating where the blond had gripped the little one.

"Ahhhh," Declan murmured, nodding slowly. "I remember that. Ye saw me with Page. She banged up her arm." His expression appeared a little vacant, his eyes narrowing, as he continued, "I gave Page to her mother, Samone, to carry for a bit." With a blink, Declan refocused on Thoron. "Page ended up fine after a few minutes and joined us runnin' again."

Thoron nodded, glad to hear that the youngster didn't end up with any lasting damage. "Then you changed back and followed the rest of the pack out of sight. I figured the blond was Lark, your husband, but Aaron said he's human. Did he change after you gave him your claiming bite?" He'd wondered about that but hadn't gotten around to asking. "How long does it take to turn into a shifter after you're claimed?"

Declan's smile turned a little amused, and he peered at Aaron who'd been sitting on a nearby sofa, watching silently. "It looks like ye still have a few things to explain."

"A lot, actually," Aaron admitted, his expression rueful. "There's always plenty to explain when introducing a human to the paranormal world."

"That there is," Declan agreed. Returning his focus to Thoron, he told him, "A shifter claiming ye does not turn ye into a shifter, too. While ye'll get a few enhancements . . . more strength, speed, better health, ye'll always be human." Sobering, Declan pointed toward the study door. "Ye'll want to be sure to use our pack doctors as opposed to general practitioners, however, because anomalies can show up in bloodwork that would be tough to explain."

Thoron nodded, understanding. "Got it."

"Okay, then." Declan reached over and patted Thoron on the shoulder. "Thank ye for the information. I'm glad it wasn't any of me people bein' careless." His lips curving into a wry smile, Declan pushed away from the table. "You just happen to enjoy bein' in the deep woods. We'll have to watch for others like that, too."

"I stopped looking for you all after that," Thoron admitted as he crossed to stand next to Aaron, who'd also risen. Shoving his hands in his jeans' pockets, Thoron shrugged. "I mean, you're the head park ranger. I've worked with you. I knew you weren't a danger to anyone, so I figured you were just a hidden society not hurting anyone." Seeing Declan's dark brows rising on his forehead, Thoron scoffed. "Hell, it wasn't any of my business."

"And now, it is." Declan grinned as he pointed his finger between Thoron and Aaron. "Because ye're part of this world now." With a shrug, he started toward the door, saying, "Or ye will be once ye let Aaron claim ye."

Thoron felt a rush of heat to his neck, threatening to rise into his cheeks. He knew Declan was referring to sex. His ass clenched just at the idea, even as his dick plumped in his jeans.

"No rush, my mate," Aaron rumbled, rubbing his lower back. He'd leaned close as they followed the alpha out of the study and back toward the living room. "We'll get there when you're ready."

Clearing his throat, Thoron offered Aaron a small smile, but he didn't comment on that. Instead, he asked, "Would now be a good time for you to show me your rhino?" Seeing Aaron's surprised look, he added, "We dropped Tommy off for a play date at Cliff and Lisa's to play with Abigail and Lily, so I'm sure he'd appreciate a little extra time to play with the girls."

Aaron grinned. "I'd love to show you my animal form." Then he sobered. "It won't bother you to see me shift, will it?"

Thoron scoffed, shaking his head. "No. I've seen the wolves change. I know what it entails."

At first, Thoron had thought the sounds of their muscles popping and snapping, along with the sight of their skin rippling, had been a bit grotesque. After seeing them change several times, however, he realized it must not actually hurt them. They certainly didn't seem any the worse for wear for it.

"Okay. Good." Aaron led Thoron out the back door onto a massive deck. "It really does feel like a really great stretch . . . like after you've been sitting too long . . . no matter what it sounds like."

Nodding, Thoron took Aaron at his word. They headed to the back edge of the clearing. When Aaron started undressing, Thoron felt his mouth go dry. The man was just too sexy for words—big, broad, and muscular with a killer tan.

And no tan lines.

Maybe that's a shifter thing.

Aaron met his gaze and winked. Then he crouched in the grass and began to change. Aaron's change wasn't nearly instantaneous like Declan's, but he did morph pretty quickly.

Within a matter of ten to fifteen seconds, Aaron's human form expanded and thickened. Horns appeared on his growing head, and a tail appeared. His skin thickened and darkened, turning an almost grayish color.

Finally, a large rhinoceros stood before Thoron.

"Wow," Thoron whispered, unable to help himself. "You're . . . magnificent."

The animal appeared almost to preen before lumbering slowly toward Thoron. Holding his ground, he watched Aaron in animal form close the few feet between them. Then the rhino rubbed the side of his massive head against Thoron's hip.

With a chuckle, Thoron rested his hands on the beast's head. He rubbed over the slightly bumpy hide, and a bubble of laughter erupted from his throat. Thoron refused to call it a giggle.

Still, almost giddy with elation, Thoron rubbed his hands over the rhino, exploring his huge frame. The animal was almost six feet at the shoulder and a good twelve feet from the tip of his big horn to the end of his wide body. Thoron sure appreciated that Aaron was sentient, making him careful where he stepped because Thoron would never want to be trod on by his huge feet.

A few minutes later, a pack of a half dozen wolves joined them, and the group began to play.

Thoron made his way to the back deck, out of the way. Lark joined him and handed him a glass with a pale pink liquid in it. Taking a sniff, Thoron tried to figure out what it was.

Lark chuckled. "Pink lemonade."

"Ah. Thanks." Thoron lifted the glass in a small salute, making the ice cubes clink. Then he took a deep gulp of the bittersweet drink. Humming appreciatively, Thoron welcomed the coolness on his tongue and throat. Then he settled in to watch the wolves play with Aaron's rhino. "They do this often?" he asked curiously.

Nodding, Lark grinned as he eyed the group. "Quite a bit, yeah," he confirmed. "Shifters, in general, are really quite affectionate while in animal form."

"Cool." Thoron didn't know what else to say, so he just sat and watched.

After a while, the wolves took off running into the woods, and Aaron returned to human form. He quickly pulled on his clothes and made his way to Thoron's side. Leaning down, Aaron pressed a quick, hard kiss to Thoron's lips.

"That was fun," Aaron told him with a grin. "Thanks for your patience."

"Not a problem," Thoron replied honestly. He held up his glass, offering the drink to his lover. "It was interesting to watch."

Aaron took the drink and swallowed several gulps. Just as he handed the glass back, Declan exited the house with another man following.

"Guys, I'd like to introduce ye to Clancy Strobeman." Declan indicated the blond man with him. "He's our pack's current child custody lawyer and will be handlin' yer case against Janelle."

"Really?" Worry filled Thoron. "But I can't pay—"

"He's pack, Thoron," Declan cut in. "The pack will finance him, so don't ye worry. Now, I know Janelle ended up in jail last night, but ye weren't certain if ye were pressin' charges."

"You should definitely press charges," Clancy told them. "It'll help. It'll give us grounds to petition a judge to have Tommy placed with you on an emergency basis."

Thoron arched his brows. "Really?"

"Really." Clancy grinned. "Janelle can't very well care for Tommy if she's cooling her jets in a jail cell, right?"

"But I'm still a single father and firefighter with shit hours," Thoron pointed out. "My situation really hasn't changed."

No matter how much he wanted Tommy with him.

"Your situation has changed," Aaron countered, sliding his arm around his waist. "You have me now, and the pack's help." He winked. "Which means all kinds of daycare, play-dates, and friends options."

"Wow."

Thoron whispered the word, feeling a little overwhelmed. It finally hit him. With Aaron by his side, he not only gained a dedicated lover and partner, but a whole new kind of family.

Now I just have to figure out how to accept his claim.

CHAPTER NINE

After three days of living and sleeping beside his mate, Aaron was afraid he would die of blue balls. He'd promised his lover time, though, and no matter what, he would do it. His mate was worth any pain or price.

Besides, it wasn't as if they didn't do anything together. They'd shared showers where they'd jerked each other off. Every evening ended with mutual blowjobs or hand jobs. The kissing was damn near off the charts whenever Tommy wasn't in the room.

While Tommy was a little confused as to why Mommy hadn't come to pick him up the next day like usual, he was enjoying his time with his father. Aaron liked the time with Tommy, too, reading together, playing trucks, and building towers out of blocks. When Thoron had gone back to work that morning, Aaron had been a little nervous to be taking care of Tommy alone, but he'd managed it just fine.

Tommy's a good kid.

Aaron would be starting his own part-time work firefighting soon, and he worried about how he would manage working with his unclaimed mate. His instinct to care for and see to Thoron's health rode him hard. If he claimed him, Aaron knew it would be easier because his mate would have the perks of being bonded to a shifter.

Time. It'll happen.

The front door opened, and Aaron walked into the house.

Tommy slid from the chair at the dining room table where they'd been coloring, yelling, "Daddy!" He streaked across the room, and Thoron crouched to catch him.

"Hey, buddy," Thoron greeted, hugging him. "How was your day?"

"Good. We played blocks and cars, and now we're coloring." Tommy tugged on Thoron's hand. "Come see what I drew."

Thoron dutifully joined them at the table, *oohing* and *aahing* over his son's picture.

Aaron waited patiently until Thoron finished with Tommy. Then he moved in for his own kiss. It was just a short peck, but seeing, scenting, and touching Thoron helped settle him. Aaron could still smell a hint of fire on Thoron's skin, telling him he'd been working hard. The scent of soap was there, too, and he knew Thoron had had time to scrub afterward.

"Welcome home, babe," Aaron greeted softly before giving him a second kiss. "I have a casserole in the oven. Should be ready in about twenty minutes."

"That sounds wonderful, Aaron." Thoron gave him a soft look, something twinkling in his dark eyes. "Thank you."

Aaron was tempted to ask what that look was for, but he resisted. While Tommy was used to seeing them together, they didn't talk about their relationship in front of him. All the boy knew was that Aaron was Daddy's boyfriend, and the kid seemed good with that.

After Tommy had been read his bedtime story and was fast asleep in bed, Aaron stood brushing his teeth in the ensuite. He heard Thoron in the bedroom and looked forward to getting some alone time with him. His cock hardened in anticipation, and he hurried to spit and rinse.

Before Aaron could turn away from the sink, Thoron came in and wrapped his arms around him from behind. He nuzzled the back of Aaron's neck, mouthing kisses along the tendon of his neck. Tipping his head to the side, Aaron moaned softly as tingles trickled down his chest, making his nipples bead.

"Thoron," Aaron whispered softly, knowing they needed to keep it down. "Feels so good."

"Hmmm," Thoron hummed as he mapped Aaron's chest with his fingers. "Always feel so good."

Finding Aaron's hard nipples, Thoron pinched and rolled them.

Groaning, Aaron allowed his head to drop back on Thoron's shoulder as goose bumps broke out over his arms. He reached back with his right hand and gripped his mate's hip. Resting his second hand on Thoron's strong arm, Aaron basked in the attention of his mate as his human explored every inch of his torso.

His stomach fluttered, and his abdominals twitched. His cock throbbed in his sweats. Even his balls ached in the best of ways.

"I have a surprise for you, Aaron," Thoron purred into his ear before giving the lobe a suckle.

Gasping, Aaron felt a bead of pre-cum ooze from his prick. "Wh-What?" he asked breathlessly, barely able to get the one word out.

"Come to bed, and I'll show you."

Thoron eased his arms from around Aaron, taking his hand. As Aaron turned to follow his guiding mate, he spotted the hungry expression on his human's face. His eyes were narrowed a bit, and his pupils were dilated. Thoron peered over his shoulder at him while leading him out of the bathroom, and his gaze raked over him with heat.

Aaron felt a full body shudder work through him as another bead of pre-cum slipped from him.

"Thoron," Aaron murmured. A glance toward the door

showed it was closed. He even noticed it was locked. Arching one brow, Aaron refocused on Thoron. "What's going on?"

Thoron had never locked the door before, just in case Tommy needed something.

"I'll unlock it later," Thoron replied by way of explanation. "Right now, I want to show you my surprise."

Aaron watched as Thoron tucked the thumb of his free hand into the waistband of his sweats. He pulled the fabric forward, then pushed it down. With a twitch of his hips, Thoron's sweats fell to the floor.

Spotting Thoron's long, slender dark erection, Aaron's mouth watered. The bead of pre-cum gleaming on his flared head almost had him hitting his knees for a taste. Only the squeeze of Thoron's fingers against his own stayed the reaction and had him lifting his gaze to Thoron's face.

"Not tonight, Aaron," Thoron told him, heat gleaming in his eyes. "Tonight, I want something else."

"Anything," Aaron instantly replied.

Finally, a hint of nerves filled Thoron's scent.

It was Aaron's turn to squeeze Thoron's hand. With his other, he cradled his mate's nape as he drew close. Their bodies only a hairsbreadth apart, Aaron could feel the heat of the other man.

"Tell me, my mate," Aaron encouraged. "What do you need?"

If it was within Aaron's power, he would make it happen . . . no matter what.

"I've been stretching," Thoron told him, his voice soft and husky. "Getting myself ready for you."

Aaron felt his brows shoot up. "Really?" A burst of need slammed through him, and his cock twitched.

Thoron nodded once. His gaze was intense as he peered into Aaron's eyes. "I want you to claim me, my shifter."

Moaning deep in his throat, Aaron shuddered, his blood

burning in his veins. "I want that," he murmured huskily. Drawing in a deep breath, he tried to settle himself. "More than anything."

A sensual smile curved Thoron's full lips, and his eyes grew heavy-lidded. "Then come claim me." As he spoke, he drew away from Aaron and climbed onto the bed.

Aaron's attention fell to the firm globes of Thoron's ass, and as he moved, something else caught his attention. He took a step toward the bed as another gasp escaped his lips. His mate had a pale green plug in his ass.

"Thoron," Aaron whispered, pressing the heel of his palm to the base of his dick. His cock spurted a burst of pre-cum, and he moaned again as Thoron settled on his knees and elbows, his legs spread. "Oh, fuck me."

"Other way around, Aaron." Thoron grinned over his shoulder at him. "I need you." He wiggled his ass. "Claim me?"

Not liking the question in his tone, Aaron vowed to erase it quick, fast, and in a hurry. He shucked his own sweats, then reached for the nightstand drawer, intending to get the lube. Instead, Aaron spotted the bottle already out on the nightstand.

Snatching it up, Aaron hurried to join his lover on the bed. His hands shook as he popped the cap and poured a liberal amount on his fingers. He tossed the lube onto the bed, then rested his clean hand on Thoron's back.

"Damn, babe," Aaron muttered, trying to get himself under control. "Never would have guessed."

As Aaron rubbed his palm up and down Thoron's spine, massaging the knobs, a tremble of anticipation worked through him.

"Wanted you from the start," Thoron told him, his voice soft and quiet as he held Aaron's gaze over his shoulder. "Just daunted by your size."

Aaron understood and nodded. "Thank you for your gift."

As Aaron spoke, he slid his hand down Thoron's trench and carefully gripped the base of the plug. He gently eased it out, finding it larger than he'd expected. Tossing it to the bed, Aaron quickly replaced it with his lubed fingers, easily sliding in the first two.

Thoron arched beneath him, rocking into his touch. "More, Aaron," he urged, his tone demanding. "I'm ready. I need more."

Obeying his mate, Aaron pushed a third finger in beside the other two. He crooked his fingers, searching for that pleasure nub. Hearing Thoron's soft grunt, feeling his tremble, Aaron knew he'd found it.

"Fuuuuuck," Thoron hissed. "Now."

Aaron's cock throbbed as he listened to Thoron's words and felt the tremors working through his body as he stroked over his back with his other hand. Needing just as badly as Thoron, he slipped his fingers out. After swiping the lube over his erection, gritting his teeth to keep from blowing just at that simple stimulation, Aaron guided his dick to Thoron's prepared hole.

Touching his crown to Thoron's entrance caused a shiver to work up Aaron's spine. He gripped the base of his dick tightly for control, then pushed. His flared head popped past his mate's guardian muscles and was enveloped in the sweet, gripping heat of his mate.

Groaning, Aaron froze when Thoron clenched. He stared down at where he finally penetrated his mate, his abdominals clenching with the pleasure of it. After several racing heartbeats, where Aaron rubbed a hand over Thoron's back soothingly, his mate's body relaxed.

Letting out a long breath, Aaron levered over Thoron. He rested his weight on his left hand as he wrapped his right arm around his waist. Holding his mate tightly, Aaron pressed forward, sinking deep into Thoron's body in one long, smooth glide.

Buried balls deep, Aaron paused. He rested his forehead against Thoron's nape, breathing in his mate's heady scent—a mixture of sweat, man, and arousal.

"Move, Aaron," Thoron pleaded. "I need."

"I'll give you what you need, my mate," Aaron vowed. Then he began to move.

Aaron eased most of the way out before thrusting back inside, keeping his strokes slow and measured. On each one, he adjusted his angle slightly. Finally, on the fifth stroke, Aaron felt it and heard it.

Thoron groaned deep in his throat as a tremble worked through him.

Found it.

Having found Thoron's prostate, Aaron sped up his strokes. Faster and faster, he pegged his mate's pleasure button. The feel of Thoron's body shaking beneath him spurred Aaron on, needing to make his mate fly.

Then Thoron was there.

Thoron shoved his fist in his mouth to stifle his scream as his body contracted around Aaron's cock.

Clenching his jaw, Aaron managed another few strokes before the sweet pressure became too much. He plunged deep and stilled, his balls pulling tight as he poured his release into his lover's channel. His teeth ached for a new reason as his rhino bellowed in his mind.

Ancient instincts took hold, and Aaron opened his mouth and sank his teeth into Thoron's neck. The delicious nectar of his mate's life-giving fluid flowed across his tongue, lighting up his taste buds. He groaned as he sucked, searching for more.

As Aaron swallowed the iron-rich fluid, he felt Thoron shudder once more as his mate pitched over that precipice again.

Smiling with satisfaction, Aaron eased his teeth from Thoron's flesh and licked over the wound, sealing it and leaving his mark on his mate. After kissing it once, twice, he eased them to their left, keeping them flush, with his dick still embedded in his mate.

Thoron let out a long, low breath. "Wow," he mumbled.

Aaron let out his own satisfied sigh. "Yeah." He kissed his mate's neck again. "Wow." A heartbeat later, he whispered, "Thank you, my mate."

Turning his head a little, Thoron graced him with a loopy grin. "No, thank you."

After kissing the corner of Thoron's mouth awkwardly, Aaron relaxed back on the bed. "I know we need to clean up and dress, but let me hold you like this for just a few minutes."

Thoron rested in Aaron's arms, cuddling against him. "Sounds perfect."

A moment later, Aaron heard the sound of Thoron's soft snores, and he grinned.

I'll clean us up in just a few minutes.

CHAPTER TEN

A few days later, Thoron watched Aaron wash the side of the fire truck. Every move he made accentuated his hard, muscular ass. Thoron barely resisted walking over and smacking it.

"If you stare any harder, his pants'll start on fire."

Hearing Paolo's teasing, Thoron looked the shifter's way and smirked. "Funny man."

Ever since allowing Aaron to claim him, Thoron had felt more at ease, more settled. The guys had seemed to accept him more, had opened up, and relaxed around him. Thoron had never noticed how guarded some of them were around him, always watching what they said, how they moved, or tempering their strength so he didn't see just how strong they were.

Not anymore.

Now they openly joked and laughed, teasing him about Aaron, sex, and making exaggerated sniffing motions.

They really were a goofy bunch.

Paolo opened his mouth, probably to make another quip, but the sound of the alarm beat him to it. Everyone jumped into action. They slung on their gear and piled onto the truck.

Dolan, a fellow firefighter mated with a wolf shifter, drove the truck. He expertly navigated the streets, taking them up a winding road. An old two-story farmhouse was already well ablaze.

Unloading, Thoron knew the structure was already a complete loss. He unrolled a hose and started spraying the area around the flaming building. There were a number of out-buildings, including a barn, a woodshed, a shop, and a storage shed. They would do their best to save them.

Brahms headed over to the couple standing off to the side, cuddling with each other while holding a crying boy of maybe twelve years. Thoron couldn't make out what was said, but he saw him nod. Then Brahms jogged back toward them.

"No one is inside, thank the gods," Brahms told everyone. "Keep the hoses on the ground and douse the outbuildings. Let's keep this contained, gentlemen."

Just as Brahms finished speaking, a loud pop filled the air. A burning timber flew through the air and landed on the roof of the barn. The dry roofing instantly caught.

"Shit," Dolan snarled. He moved his hose and began trying to contain it.

"Our horses and milk cow are in there," the man called, making a move as if to head that way.

"Stay back, sir," Brahms called. Pointing at Thoron and Aaron, he ordered, "Let 'em loose." Then he took over Aaron's hose.

Paolo continued spraying the other buildings and the ground while Dolan and Brahms concentrated on the barn.

Thoron rushed toward the still-burning barn, Aaron on his heels. Reaching the barn first, he threw the latch and opened the doors wide. He followed Aaron inside and swept his gaze over the interior.

The scream of upset animals coupled with the crackle of the fire filled the air, making his eardrums ring. The large pole barn was divided into several pens with moveable panels. He tried to figure out where the gates were, but the smoke in the air made it tough to figure out the people's rhyme or reason to the configuration.

After a few seconds of confusion, Thoron pulled his fire axe and began hacking at the rope that was holding two panels together. He quickly swung one panel to the side, doing his best to stay out of the way of the frightened horse within. The animal bolted past him, clipping his shoulder, but he didn't go down.

Ow. That'll bruise.

Thoron looked around once more, noticing Aaron had done something similar with another pen.

The bellow of a cow drew Thoron's attention to the back where another pen had been set up for their milk cow. Maneuvering between panels, he hurried that way. He opened the barn's rear door first, then turned back to the pen.

Aaron was already there opening it.

Stepping to the side, Thoron cleared the way for the animal to gallop passed. He began to turn when he saw Aaron freeze while still in the barn. His lover seemed to be looking past him, but he made no effort to exit the still-burning barn.

"Aaron?" Thoron called through his helmet. Then he turned and spotted what had Aaron's attention. "What the hell?"

Janelle stood ten feet away from Thoron. In her hand was a gun, and she was pointing it right at him. A calculating smile curved her lips, and a cold gleam filled her green eyes. She'd been released on bail several days before, but with Tommy having been ordered to stay in Thoron's care until her charges were settled, he hadn't seen her.

"This is just perfect," Janelle stated with a grin. "When I set the last couple of fires and waited and watched, I was going to settle for just you, Thoron, but now I get both queers at the same time."

Ripping off his helmet, Thoron asked, "What the hell are you doing, Janelle?" He took a step toward her.

Janelle fired a shot at Thoron's feet, making him jump back. "No, no, no. Stay there." Then she smirked. "In fact, head on back into the barn with the other one."

Thoron took a step backward as he frowned. "What do you

want?"

"For you to die," Janelle stated as if it was the most obvious thing in the world.

Maybe it should have been.

"Why?" Thoron demanded. "Is this about custody of Tommy? Or me being bisexual?"

"Bisexual isn't a thing," Janelle insisted. "You're either normal or a pervert." Her lips curved into a sneer. "And since you're a pervert and someone who got money for a lawyer, I think I want it."

Thoron couldn't believe what he was hearing. "This is about money?" She'd always liked to ask for extra cash above and beyond his child support payments, but he never would have guessed she would stoop to this level.

"Well, that and I can't have a pervert near my son." Janelle shrugged a shoulder negligently. "Anyway, I'm sure you haven't bothered to update your will since you hooked up with that other pervert, so everything will come to me." Scoffing, Janelle rolled her eyes. "You always were bad about updating paperwork."

That was true. Thoron was bad about paperwork. Janelle was right, too. In the event of his death, everything he had would go to her so she could use it to take care of Tommy.

Except, Thoron had something to live for. He glanced over his shoulder, wondering what Aaron was thinking about all this. Thoron swept his gaze over the hazy gloom, but he didn't see him.

"Where'd he go?" Janelle demanded. Obviously, she'd been just as distracted. "Damn it," she screeched. "Where is he?" Then Janelle cackled—actually *cackled*. "Your lover left you to die. How funny!" Lifting the gun, she commented, "But since I can't have you leaving . . ."

The ground beneath Thoron's feet trembled, and he stumbled. The bellow of a rhinoceros filled the air as the large animal galloped past him. Thoron grabbed the door, barely keeping on his feet as the ground shuddered from the impact of the big animal's feet.

Janelle screamed.

The report of a gun filled the air over and over.

The thud of a body hitting another reached Thoron. When he managed to right himself enough to look over, he saw his ex-wife flying through the air. She crashed to the ground in a heap, and Aaron's rhino was soon at her side.

Thoron ran for the pair. Skidding to stop beside Aaron, he rested his hand on Aaron's rhino's shoulder. Janelle's leg stuck out at an odd angle, but he was pretty sure he saw her chest moving, indicating she was still breathing.

"Easy, babe," Thoron soothed, feeling the animal shudder with what was probably barely leashed aggression. "Just relax."

When Thoron stepped forward, intending to check the pulse of the prone woman, the rhino moved between them.

Looking into Aaron's big gray eye, Thoron told him, "I need to see if she's alive, babe." He rubbed over his lover's front horn, trying to get him to relax. "We'll have to call the cops."

After a long moment, Aaron took a step back, allowing Thoron to pass. He crouched down and felt for a pulse. He found it. Feeling around Janelle's head, he discovered an impressive knot, which would most likely be the cause of why she was unconscious.

"Hey. What happened?" Brahms called, jogging toward them. "Is that your ex?"

He'd obviously spotted Janelle.

"Yeah," Thoron confirmed. He heard the sound of Aaron shifting, so he began shucking his coveralls for him to put on. "She tried to trap us in the barn to make it look like we'd died in the fire." Shaking his head, Thoron straightened and held out his pants to a now-human Aaron. "Insurance money and to get rid of queers. Didn't realize she was bigoted until I started dating Aaron."

"Are you okay?" Aaron asked, grabbing Thoron and starting to pat him down.

"I'm fine," Thoron assured, looking over Aaron's partially covered frame. "I should be asking you that. How did she not shoot you?"

"She did shoot me," Aaron claimed, causing Thoron to gasp. His lover grinned and winked. "That caliber bullet won't penetrate my rhino's hide."

"Damn it," Thoron snapped. "You scared the shit out of me."

"Sorry, babe," Aaron murmured contritely before taking his mouth in a deep kiss.

When they came up for air, Brahms told them, "I called the cops. Deputy Nereo is on his way. He'll take care of all this." He waved his hand to indicate the gaping couple and their son, as well as Janelle.

"Oops." Aaron ducked his head, his cheeks taking on a pinkish hue.

Brahms laughed. "Don't worry about it. We've handled worse." With a wink, he added, "Nereo's a vampire, so he'll be able to alter a few memories so no one remembers the big ass rhino." Brahms patted Aaron's wide shoulder.

Thoron froze, his jaw sagging open. "Vampires are real?" he asked on a gasp.

Brahms barked a laugh, shaking his head as he walked away.

Aaron pulled Thoron into a tight hug, holding him snugly against his bare chest. "I still have a lot to tell you about," he murmured into Thoron's ear before bussing a kiss to his temple. "You still have a lot to learn about the paranormal world, babe."

"I guess I do," Thoron whispered in awe.

But I'll get there . . . with Aaron by my side.

As they started walking back around the smoldering but still standing barn, Thoron couldn't think of anything better in the world.

A future with my shifter.

ABOUT THE AUTHOR

Charlie started writing fantasy when she was eight, and after stumbling onto her first erotic romance at age nineteen, she realized her true calling. She now focuses on writing gay erotic romance, normally of the paranormal variety, with heroes of all kinds. With the help and support of her husband, Charlie finally fulfilled one of her life-long goals . . . move to acreage with her horses. You can often find her curled up with her laptop and a cup of tea or glass of wine, creating her next adventure. Charlie enjoys exploring the mountains of her new Oregon home on horseback, 4-wheeler, or motorcycle.

She can be reached at ch.richards2010@yahoo.com
Or visit her at www.charlie-richards.com.

www.ingramcontent.com/pod-product-compliance
Lightning Source LLC
Chambersburg PA
CBHW070537130626
46555CB00003B/1472